Cindy -

FROM A GATHERING OF

Glass

We are all formed from but a gathering of glass —

Rah Mog

FROM A GATHERING OF Glass

ROBIN MOYER

Wynwidyn PRESS

PINCKNEY, MI

For information
regarding permission, write to:

Wynwidyn Press, LLC
Attention: Permissions Department
425 Rose, Pinckney, Michigan, 48169

ISBN: 978-1-941737-12-5

Editing by Karen Elizabeth Bush
www.lexiconsvs.com

Cover Art by Darren Wheeling
Layout Design by Donna Shubel
Cover Photography by Robin Moyer

Dedication

For the dragonflies and caterpillars and emerging butterflies, for everyone who blooms and blossoms into their true selves, for everyone who continues to grow and reach toward being the best and brightest they can possibly be!

Robin

Ribbons

Once unraveled, fraying,
twisted into knots of uncertainty
yet never tying anything together.
Once trodden into dirt pathways
that led nowhere,
then everywhere.
Ribbons rewoven into glass,
given structure,
tears melting into smiles
as a family gathers.
Now ribbons tie us together
with bows blossoming as
family grows
with ties that bind
and free.

~Joshua VanAllen

Prologue: FOUNDING

Peter read the note he would leave behind. He knew his father would be upset, but he didn't think he'd order him to come back home. He was pursuing a career in a form of art after all – just not quite what his father had envisioned when he'd paid for Peter's college earning him a degree as an art historian.

Father,
I have taken the money Grandmother Alice left for me and am off to learn the art of glassblowing. This is what I need to do. It's what I want to do. You've always felt the desire to critique; I have always felt the need to create. We each need to do what will make us happy. There was a reason I took so many classes having to do with both the history and the execution of the many styles of glass blowing. Now I will be able to put my visions to work creating. I'll be back in the states when I've learned what I must learn and done what I must do.
    Peter

Peter shrugged as he folded the paper and slid it into an

envelope. Didn't matter what he'd written really. His father would not be happy, but then it seemed that no matter what Peter did, it didn't please his father. It didn't matter as much anymore. Peter smiled as he put the envelope on his father's desk. Just the thought of the journey ahead filled him with joy and excitement.

He was off to the Abate Zanetti Glass School in Venice, Italy. Thank God for Grandmother Alice, the grandmother he'd never met – who wasn't really even his grandmother – but who had left him enough money to go after his dreams.

He grabbed his almost empty duffle bag with his new passport and his journal tucked inside and headed off to go do some shopping before going to the airport. It was time for new beginnings, a new life out on his own. It was time to be who he was.

PART One : THE GATHER

ROBIN MOYER ⌒

Chapter 1
TWO YEARS LATER

Josh wrapped his arm around Emily's shoulders as they stood in front of their newly remodeled gallery. They'd done well enough over the past three years to buy the building they were standing in. While the couple had considered moving the gallery to a new location, they loved the area where they were and, when the owner offered to sell it to them, they jumped at the chance.

Removing walls and floors from the old building had created a two story central atrium surrounded on three sides by long galleries. A long, curved staircase wound around the central atrium, leading to the second floor where smaller, more intimate rooms would soon house smaller collections.

"We've done it, Joshua. It looks far more like a home than a typical art gallery now with the grand parlor to the right and the library to the left. The walls in the atrium will showcase our larger works, and yet our guests will feel as if they're in a home, able to imagine bringing the pieces into their *own* homes.

"The new sign should be here tomorrow." A cry from the yard had Emily turning to see the three children in a tumbled pile wrestling in the front yard of The Gallery.

"Children!" admonished Emily. "Your clothes!! It's too early in the day to be covered in grass stains and mud!"

"Emmy, Ally, watch out for your sister. You have to remember Journey isn't as big as you both are," cautioned Josh. "She's only three. Come on, let's go look at our new home."

Together, the family walked down the short walkway around to the back of the gallery. The addition there would become their new home: three bedrooms, a large living area and kitchen, and a screened-in porch leading to a deck overlooking the bay. Above it, the rear windows of the gallery soared.

Josh left his wife and the children to settle into their new quarters and returned to the gallery alone. Walking through the tall, carved wooden double doors into the small entry area before the atrium, he ran his fingers gently along the old schoolmaster's desk that served as a reception area, as well as the place for patrons to pay for their purchases.

On the wall behind the desk hung the painting Josh had painted of Aokigahara, and to its right, the framed calligraphy poem. The painting was one of his best. In it, sunlight beamed down through a canopy of closely growing trees. Trailings of ribbons wove their way into the distance. Rather than being dark or foreboding, a sense of light and hope emanated from the painting. It was something they would never sell, for it was a picture of their journey to Jukai and reflected all the positives they had learned along the way.

As he wandered back toward the central area, Josh ran his fingers through his long, tawny-blond hair. His moss-green eyes looked up and up to the ceiling, to the tall, narrow windows rising above the first landing.

"There needs to be a sculpture or chandelier hanging there. Something big and light that makes a statement," he thought. Maybe the glass artist coming in next week might have something that would work. He'd heard about her ("Piper" he thought her name was) from friends who had seen some of her pieces. She was new to the area and was just settling into to her new studio, having been an apprentice glass blower in Venice for several years. Josh was looking forward to seeing her work in person. Curving off to the left, Josh entered the long gallery where some artwork was already hanging. This room held primarily the work of an artist/photographer he'd come across online, and whom he'd convinced to let him be her west coast source.

He liked her work because she had a way with charcoal and did excellent (whether stark or ethereal) black and white photography – something one just didn't see much of anymore. Her work had captivated him, pulling him in to her worlds. She was extremely creative and all her images let seers add their own experiences to them. The most striking aspect of her work was that no two people ever seemed to "see" exactly the same thing. Another intriguing aspect of her pieces was the way she matted or framed them. She had a tendency to employ the unusual for that, from needlepoint hoops to apple crates – or having the art itself become a frame enclosing a space for yet undrawn possibilities.

Scattered around were matted pieces of the same artist's poetry, done in calligraphy on rice paper when they 'went with' a particular piece, or printed on top of the delicate water color paintings which, with one exception, were the only pop of color in the room.

There were still pedestals and long, low seating to be installed where they would create a path that allowed the visitor to focus on one piece at a time.

At the far end of the room, in front of and blocking the single, large window was a watercolor painting. It was at once magical and fantastical or vaguely threatening, depending upon the light. In it was a sprite caught in an autumnal moment, a seasoned faery clothed in oak leaves or dreams, depending upon the viewer's angle. According to several of Josh's friends who had seen it, her look either was all-knowing, or puzzled, or self-satisfied – and it was that disagreement about her expression that had people talking about and questioning what exactly a "Thevri" even was. It was sure to be one of the highlights of the Grand Opening in a few weeks, and the question it posed was put in so many words in the advertising that even now was heralding the big event.

The artist, the elusive (as he thought of her) C.M. Baker, was vaguely responsive to his insistence that she come for the grand opening. He hoped she'd come; he wanted her to. But, he didn't figure he could or would know for sure unless and until she actually showed up.

Josh wandered back to the parlor on the other side of the entrance. Here, two couches flanked a large fireplace midway down the far wall. At the end of the room, French doors led to a large terrace, scattered with wrought-iron tables and chairs and potted plants, and boasting a view of the bay over the roof of their home below.

In the parlor itself there were baskets created by fine Maidu artisans. These baskets rested on low wooden tables, so it was easy to see the deer and elk, running cats and flying eagles that were woven into the basketry patterns. There were displays of feathered ceremonial head plumes, beaded aprons and Maidu handmade dolls. Glass shadowboxes hung on the walls above where they displayed turquoise bracelets and amulets, bone combs and ceremonial dress. On other walls hung stick rattles, ceramic tribal masks and paintings. Pottery samples were sometimes low and wide and sometimes tall and slender. All were displayed in tall, glassed-in boxes on carved, wooden pedestals. Woven blankets draped across the backs of couches. A Maidu drum was placed so that anyone might feel free to let the drum speak.

It was a good space and he'd made arrangements to acquire some Maidu music to be played softly at certain times during the day.

Standing out on the balcony now, he appreciated how the Thevri art was accessible from this side of the glass as well as the other. With the display covering the whole window as it did, what one saw from the outside seemed arrestingly different than it did from the inside. Different parts were emphasized in a way that the two sides of the glass made up the whole of the display. It all gave the viewer a totally different, totally engaging experience.

Winding around to the atrium, Joshua paused halfway up the stairs and thought again about the need for something to take up or emphasize that space. Did anyone do work that massive? Would someone buy such a thing if he or she did? It would be, he knew, the sort of piece that if one had to ask the price, chances were the questioner could not afford to pay it. Yet, that space almost demanded some sort of a statement piece.

Continuing upward, he went into the first of three smaller rooms that were placed back to back to back. The archways between them were staggered so that one could not take a straight path through them. The first room was primarily Josh's own artwork, things inspired by Emily and his children. Reflections and refractions of each other, the paintings were placed in such a way that, while they appeared to be mirror images, upon closer inspection the paintings were of entirely different-looking people viewed through a multitude of remembered, imagined or emotional filters.

The middle room was devoted to Jukai, always Jukai. The forest still had him in its grasp, although now, it was a constant source of inspiration. He was doing a series of paintings, oils, of the "Canted Trees of Jukai" which, while he envisioned the paintings being sold as a set, he would happily sell individually as well. Made all of bent knees and twisted elbows, roots entangled with the boughs, vine-like tendrils ensnaring the branches, the trees of Jukai were at once a puzzle to be solved and a maze to be wandered. Another of his works was a series of smaller paintings linked by multiple varicolored ribbons stretching all along one of the walls.

The third room, empty now and waiting hopefully for the works of the glass artist, was of glass on two sides and mirrored on the third, allowing for the play of light to caress and kaleidoscope off the future works within.

On the other side of the second floor were two individual rooms, one, its purpose as yet to be settled on (although possibly becoming a studio) and the other, at the back of the entire floor, served as the gallery office.

Heading into his office, Josh settled in front of the computer and pulled up the file on Piper McAllister. Pretty, twenty-something, with long, curly, auburn hair and green eyes, he thought she looked vaguely familiar, but he had no clue from where. Josh looked at several photos of her glass sculptures and remembered how he was sure, gut deep, that he needed to have her work at his gallery.

One of the sculptures was comprised of multiple spearing reaches of glass: reds and oranges at the heart of it that had morphed from greens and blues near the base, then blending, fading, and transcending into deep purples and blues at the outer edges. Somewhere between a star and an explosion, the piece, fully three feet tall, was entitled, simply, 'Day.' A companion piece, a horizontally arched wave of deep blue, purples and almost-silvers layered over a deeper, shimmering expanse of mauves, reds and deep, deep blues, was simply entitled, 'Night.'

Another glass sculpture, 'It's A Puzzle' was a series of loops, swirls, and undulating spirals: at once sinuous and sleek while tangled in and about itself.

Yet another was a large, clear, blown glass orb with a second pale, pale green orb inside it that, in turn, encased a deep crimson orb, small, no more than a few inches wide. This work she'd named 'The Heart of the Matter.'

The last one that caught his eye was entitled 'Swimming Against the Current.' Five shapes resembling jellyfish linked together by what appeared to be their tentacles.

Each piece of her art was more creative than the last and, aside from the pure art of it all, even the names of each individual piece called to the writer in him. All of her prices were far less than he knew he'd get for them here. He knew she'd only recently gotten her glass studio set up a few miles away and couldn't wait to meet her. He returned to the photo of her. Something, there was just this something there, at the very edge of his consciousness, as if he'd seen her before. Josh shook his head. It escaped him.

Chapter 2

"Never again are we moving a houseful of five people's stuff, plus a gallery full of artwork within the same week. I am exhausted." Emily flopped on the couch, looking for all the world like a discarded rag doll.

Across the room, Josh was lying on the living room floor, his head resting on his folded arms. "Never thought we'd ever get the kids down tonight. They were so wound up. Journey was the easiest; a couple of Alyndoria chapters from her new book and she was off running around with Princess Kelly on her quest in dreamland, but Emma and Alice were still arguing over who gets the top bunk this week and who got which teddy bear. They look exactly the same to me. Lord knows how they tell them apart!"

"Emma's has the missing left eye; Alice's has the worn right paw. Easy!" Emily smiled. "First night in the new place craziness, I guess. Didn't help that Emma kept insisting she saw a ghost outside."

"Yeah, I heard her. What's with that? Thank goodness, she wasn't scared. That would not have been good on the first night here!"

"She told me that we needed to let the ghost in, like it was a cat or something." Emily shook her head. "Kids," she smiled.

Josh rolled over and looked at Emily. "I think having done the remodel so we could be nearer the gallery is going to work out well. This is a good space. I don't know how you did it, but it already feels like home."

Em smiled as she stretched. "It does. I'm glad you feel it too. I think we'll need that, seeing as the next few weeks are going to be crazy getting ready for the opening. We have so much more space. Now that many of the bigger pieces are in place, I can see where best to place some of the smaller pieces. Not on the main floor, but up on the second. I'd like it if you hung the blue and green woven rug on a wall somewhere and the artist was fine with keeping the older one on the floor in the studio room while we figure out what is going to be in there for sure. Tristan's pottery mugs can be scattered around on different tables."

"While I was wandering around in the gallery this afternoon, the shelving was delivered," Josh replied. "I had them put it on the second floor since most of it will be used up there. Oh, and a new artist came by with some of her work. Fantasy acrylics. Dragons, castles. Great for kids rooms. I told her to leave a few and we'll see if we can find a good place for them."

Emily yawned. "Maybe we will end up with stuff in the studio room after all. You might have to paint in your office. Light's good in there."

Catching her yawn, Josh nodded. "Or, I could take over part of this room," he smiled at her.

"Not on your life! Sorry, hon, but I'd really like to have a living room that actually looks like a living room for a change."

"Three kids," he reminded her. "I don't think that's going to happen."

"Must you destroy the dream so quickly?" she laughed. Emily pushed herself up from the couch and slid the sliding glass door to their deck closed.

A movement off to the side caught her eye, but when she looked over, there was nothing there.

"I think Emma got to me, now I'm seeing things too. Must have been my reflection, although I don't know how it could have been," she paused and pointed, "over there."

Josh came over to stand with her. "I think we are both just really tired. Let's go to bed."

Hand in hand, they wandered upstairs and into their new bedroom. There was room here now for the king-sized poster bed she'd always wanted, and with three children, Grandma Alice's cat and the dog, none of whom had the least bit of hesitation in joining them, the king-sized mattress was going to be a wonderful change.

Curled up in the middle of the vast expanse, Emily lay with her head tucked in the nook of Josh's shoulder. The French doors allowed for a view of the Bay, the twinkling lights of the bridges looking like a flight of fireflies in the distance. Josh wrapped his arm around her and they slept. They never noticed the pale face outside the window, wistfully watching them.

Chapter 3

Piper glanced around her new glass studio. Furnaces, glory hole, annealer were all in place. Racks of pipes and pontils, shelves of glass rods and tubing and bins of colored frits were all organized. She'd found a perfect chair used by another glass blower. It had holes and hooks that were just right for a left-handed artisan. It was worn-in, shiny with use and as comfortable as if it had been made expressly for her. The brick and stone building was just large enough, and her landlord had had no issue with her having furnaces installed. The place had running water for cooling, a small bathroom and lots of light.

'Pipedreams' was officially in business! She didn't have much room for displaying her work, but as a rule, she wasn't really expecting to have anyone in her studio. She didn't like being bothered when she was working, and the glass was unforgiving of unscheduled interruptions. When the muse hit, or if she was stretching her abilities and the physics of the glass, she was completely focused and really didn't want anyone else there.

First, though, Piper had to find a place to live; she couldn't stay at 'The Broken Goose,' a local bed and breakfast, for too much longer. She was looking forward to setting up an apartment, buying all the things she needed and decorating it just for herself.

Selling almost all her work in Italy meant she'd only had to ship a few pieces back to the states. Now, displayed as they were on shelves by the front window of her studio (with the exception of the one piece that hung centered in the window), she felt they were a reasonable showing of the work she could do. The money she'd made was more than she'd expected from her last showing overseas, and selling the large hanging sculpture of what she thought of as birds swirling in flight (for her asking price!) had given her the freedom to find a nice place to live now that she was back in the states.

She'd received an email from a local gallery eager to show her work and was meeting with the owner in a couple of days. Sitting at one of her workbenches, she looked around and smiled. Not bad for being back for only two weeks, she thought, smiling.

Three stops later, she was holding the key to her new apartment. Tucked under the eaves of a hideous looking Victorian/contemporary epic fail of a remodel, it had large windows, a view of the bay from a tiny balcony (just big enough for a hammock chair and a cup of tea), a window seat, tons of bookshelves – and to top it all off, the apartment came fully furnished. The idea of trying to get furniture up three flights of stairs was daunting to say the least, and she'd fallen in love with the quirky canopied bed, the mismatched chairs in the kitchen nook and the armoire that she couldn't figure out how anyone even had gotten up there!

She'd met two of her neighbors already, and if she hadn't already made up her mind, they'd have clinched the deal.

The guy across the hall was Devon Thorn who was, as he told her in his first non-stop paragraph, gay, had a boyfriend named Augusto, a coffee fanatic who always had a pot brewing, an indie (independent) author who was actually making it writing epic fantasy novels and who loved cats, especially Hemingway, his long-haired Maine coon cat. Hemingway weighed in at thirty-plus pounds, could open doors and was terrified of the outdoors.

Piper's 'below' neighbor was Phoenix Lane, who had long, long dark hair, overly made-up eyes, and spoke with a French accent when she thought about it. Phoenix was, she'd almost whispered in a raspy voice, a model, a transplant from France by way of Bayonne, New Jersey and she hoped Piper didn't like loud music, unless, of course, it was from any Broadway show and, well, then it was absolutely fine. The rest of the people in the building were 'pretty decent' but 'a little strange' and did Piper have a crock pot that Phoenix (call me Phee) could borrow occasionally?

Piper smiled as she got in her car to go buy sheets, towels and other necessities and then move her stuff from the B&B into her cozy new abode. 'A little strange,' she smiled, remembering, and thought she'd fit in just fine.

That night, after shooing Devon out the door with his now empty pot of pasta and dishes (she needed to get some of her own somewhere) she changed into her favorite long, muslin nightgown and sat on her little balcony considering the huge cat who'd sneaked into the apartment at some point. Hemingway snored at her feet, completely at home. Piper expected that Devon would be back as soon as he figured out Hemingway had escaped. Outside the window, the lights down the hill spread out to the bay and then to the bridges in the distance. From below, she could hear Phee's musical offerings wending their way from Les Mis to Camelot.

According to Devon, Phee'd moved in six months ago, hadn't said a word to a soul until three months ago when she returned from a short trip and threw herself a party. Everyone had been invited (by engraved invitations, no less) into an apartment that apparently was furnished in faux fur, Broadway posters and more shoes than any three females needed. Everyone drank margaritas and nibbled on hors d'oeuvres for an hour or so before making excuses to leave.

Devon had then gone on to give Piper the low down on every-one else (the other four tenants) in the building. The couple across from Phee, Denny and Jo, were writers too, had had a couple of plays produced and traveled a lot. On the first floor was Stewie, the building manager who could be bought for cupcakes or chocolate, was useless at fixing anything and slept late.

Across from him was Annabelle Stewart, a sixtyish (more like seventy-ish but who's telling?) actress from 'back in the day' who was not exactly all there and kept thinking she was still acting in one of the different movies she'd been in. You never knew who'd she be from one day to the next. She had a small dog, a Bichon Frise named Dickon, loved to chit-chat, drove an ancient Lincoln (he had a reconditioned hearse himself, but hey –the price was right!), and had a penchant for whiskey sours.

Yeah, Piper thought, an eccentric bunch, and she loved it! She stood, dislodging Hemingway, went in, put on her robe, picked up the cat who had followed her, and banged on Devon' door.

Devon answered the door in a ratty, frayed green bathrobe. "Your cat, good sir," she said, handing over the boneless feline.

"I wondered where she'd gotten to," he said, shaking his head. "She sure is relaxed with you. You naughty girl," he scolded the oblivious cat who now purred, kneading her claws into his shoulder. They said good night again and Piper returned to what already felt like home.

Chapter 4

Phoenix, dressed in a vintage Laura Ashley dress, sat stiffly on the couch, knees together, hands primly folded in her lap. This was her first visit to Dr. Schedley's office and she was nervous.

"Now, er, Phoenix is it? You understand that it is required that you complete two years of counseling before you can be approved for gender reassignment surgery, do you not?"

"Yes, I do, Monsieur Doctor. I know it is unusual to switch doctors almost at the end, but my other doctor was moving to Arizona. He said he'd forward my records to you. I've been on hormone therapy now for months."

"Why don't we begin by your telling me about your childhood, family and when you realized you were a woman inside. Also, you are twenty-two, correct?"

"Yes. Well," she sighed, thinking this would just rehash old 'stuff'. "I come from a large family. I have four brothers and sisters, two of each. I'm the middle child. My brothers are older, my sisters both younger. My brother and I are roughly two years apart. My sisters came along after I was seven. We were born near the northwest coast of France in the village of Eure. My father worked in Le Havre. I remember playing in the ruins of a castle on the property where we lived. I always wanted to be the princess.

My father was transferred to the states and I lived in New Jersey until I left home. There sure aren't any castles in Jersey. We were kids. We played, we fought and we all did pretty well in school.

"I think I was first really aware of being different after my sisters came along. I'd known I was different from my brothers, but I didn't understand why or how; I just knew I wasn't like them. Right from the get-go, my sisters were treated differently. I used to love to babysit them. I'd keep changing their clothes, putting them in their fancy dresses. I wanted lace and pretty colors, not jeans and t-shirts.

"As they got older, I was always happy to get 'stuck' playing dress-up with them. I played the mother or the queen as often as the king or the dad. I liked playing the female roles. They were more comfortable. Besides, I could wear mom's heels and not get into trouble because I was keeping my baby sisters entertained. Danny and James, my brothers, always made fun of that. Their favorite nick-name for me was 'fussy-pants,' but I didn't care as long as I could spend a few hours in long dresses, pretty hats and fancy shawls."

"And how were your parents about your 'entertaining' your sisters."

"Mom didn't care. Kept the little ones busy. Dad said that I was a 'sick puppy.' He hated it and Mom and Dad fought about it some.

"When I was ten, dad tried to ship me off to an all-boys military boarding school. Major fail. I was miserable. Dad said that if Eldon Hall couldn't make a man out of me, nothing could." She smiled broadly. "He was right!"

"So you came home?"

"Yeah, they booted me out as being incorrigible and intransigent. Don't get me wrong, I loved the actual classes, but it was a very competitive atmosphere and I simply didn't know how to compete like that. The things important to them, were not important to me. The closest I came was my uniform. I hated it with a passion, but damn me if it wasn't always perfection. My shoes were like mirrors, my creases razor sharp. My brass always shone. But inside the uniform, I felt claustrophobic. I suffocated; I couldn't breathe. It was as if I were wearing masks over masks. I couldn't, wouldn't conform.

One afternoon a couple of the guys caught me crying. From then on I was teased, my locker was trashed repeatedly, and always, just under their breaths, I was called faggot or sissy or worse. For a while, I was relieved that they just thought I was gay, but then..."

"Then?"

"Then one night they raped me." Phee looked up, her eyes swimming in tears. "Four or five of them held me down, gagged me and... and... no one stopped them. They laughed. They laughed. Like it was all a big joke."

"What happened then?"

"I went to my commanding officer and reported it. Next thing I knew, I was booted out. *I* was not Eldon Hall material.

"My father yelled and screamed at me. I embarrassed him! I tried to explain but he said I was making up stories to get out of there. He wouldn't listen. He didn't care. No one listened. Luckily, my brothers never heard about it. I went back to regular school, kept my mouth shut and did whatever I was told to do. I survived. I graduated high school and got the hell out of there."

"So, are you in contact with any of your family now?"

"My mom and my sisters. Mom and dad got divorced three years ago and mom moved out here. She lives in San Jose. Vicky's going to UCLA and Ronnie is still home with Mom. My brothers work in NYC, are married and have kids, I guess. Don't really care."

"Is your mother supportive? Is she aware of your current circumstances?"

"Yeah, Mom knows. She and my sisters go shopping with me. We aren't really close, but we aren't estranged or anything either."

"How long have you been presenting yourself as female?"

"Since the day I left home. Monsieur, I am not *presenting* myself as female. I *am* a female. Just because I was in the wrong line when they were handing out body shells, doesn't mean I am male. Everything I am inside, where it truly counts, *is* female."

He nodded. "Our time is up for today. I'll see you next Monday."

Phoenix stood, and left the office. She wasn't quite sure what she thought she'd feel. She really wasn't all that keen on shrinks and counselors, but, in this case, it was a necessary evil. She shook her head. It wasn't as if there was something wrong with her head; just her body. Did they make all the rich LA ladies go to a shrink to get their crows feet erased or to suck the fat from their asses? No, they did not. How was what she wanted any different? Bureaucrats. Anything to make a dime.

Chapter 5

C.M. Baker was in the zone. She'd had an idea for a series of chiaroscuro works and the execution of them was bleeding over into every moment. She'd never been quite so aware of every shadow, every nuance of light or dark. She loved having her work in The Gallery in a room where there was only limited light and what light there was could be controlled by a timer. Being able to control light so that a viewer could see the same pieces in varying amounts of it was a dream. Light ... the hard glaring light with pristine, sharp edged shadows; the misty light of a hazy morn with blurred edges to everything ... That was the effect she was aiming for – the series, seen in varying light.

She'd never forget that day spent in the deep pine forest. It, too, was all about light, from her early morning wander in hazy dawn, sketchbook in hand, through the high, hard light arrowing through the trees at noon, to the sharply slanted shadows of the tall, straight pines spearing against the ground come late afternoon, to the blurred edges fading into twilight. She wanted, needed to capture the essence of that walk, the trees, the feelings each passing space of time brought forth.

Once, she'd have been busy scribbling words, her pen furiously capturing, playing with ideas to convey her thoughts. That day, her pen had glided, shapes forming, capturing images on paper even as she was playing with her camera, letting it grab the core, the substance until she could render it more fully in her studio.

That man at The Gallery who was showing her work really wanted her to come for the grand opening. She really didn't want to go. Sure, it'd be great for her art. People liked actually meeting the artist.

Yet, she'd found that people's opinions of a piece could be colored by contact with an artist. Good or bad, it seemed to her that the art should stand alone, that people should form an opinion based upon what they saw, what their life experiences brought to their interpretation and their gut reaction to it.

Her frame of mind was getting in the way and the sudden tenseness caused her to snap the piece of charcoal in two. She shook her head and walked away from her easel.

Her mother picked that moment to drop by the studio, hoping she wasn't interrupting.

"Nope, it's okay, Mom. I needed a break. Coffee?"

"What's the matter? Work not going well?"

"Work is going fine, or it was until I got sidetracked thinking about going to The Gallery opening. You know how I feel about things like that, but that Josh there is really pressuring me to be on hand, giving me all these 'logical' reasons for going. I don't know how to explain to him my feelings on the subject. It really isn't logical, it's emotional. I don't want to 'explain' what a particular piece is supposed to be; I want people to tell me, or each other, what they see.

"People are like sheep. They seem to need reassurance they are seeing the 'right' thing. Or, they feel something less if they look at it and see nothing. While it never bothers me exactly, if people don't 'get' it (and the majority seem to), it always leaves a bit of a hole, an emptiness, if they don't – for whatever reason."

"Not everyone will get your work, love. It's just like those reading a poem. Some readers want everything spelled out on the surface; they are too lazy to reach in, think deeper, to look beyond mere words and go wading in metaphors. It's their failing, not yours. Their experiences or lack of them cloud their perceptions. You kind of need to shrug your shoulders and focus on those who do 'get' it, who do and can appreciate your art."

"I guess," C.M. responded. "Sort of like how you like show music or country over rap."

"Exactly. Comes down to audience. Someone who loves listening to banjo picking or folk ballads might not appreciate hard rock. Everyone has differing tastes and, chances are, you are not going to touch everyone who sees your work. I think you should go. Put on your armor and go make nice and hope they buy every single piece!"

"Thanks, Mom."

"Any time. So when's this grand opening? Any other new artists going to be there?"

"Yes, apparently, Josh has a new glass artist coming in. I can't wait to see her work. She's new to the area."

"I'll look forward to seeing it too. Got to fly, have a meeting with a new author today. See you three weeks from Saturday if not before!"

"If not before," C.M. echoed with a smile. Moms!

Chapter 6

Josh went to 'Pipedreams' to see some of Piper's work and to discuss the possibility of her creating a hanging sculpture for the atrium. His jaw dropped when he stepped inside. The photographs of her work did not do them justice. He had to have them. He wanted them all!

Piper smiled as Josh's obvious pleasure. This meeting seemed like it was going to go well.

"So," Josh started when he was again able to form coherent sentences, "I would absolutely like to see your work in The Gallery. The only problem is your prices."

"Oh. They are too high?" asked Piper.

"Ah. No. Too low. Way too low. We can get well over half again higher to start. A few months down the road, you'll get two, three times as much … if not more than that!"

"Seriously?"

Josh laughed at the look on her face. "Imagine that's the look I had on my face when I walked through the door. Piper, you are seriously good. Original. Creative. You've stretched boundaries beyond what I thought could be done with glass! Your work evokes a visceral reaction. Placed to take advantage of the lighting, where each piece can command its own space, they will be breathtaking!

Those green, green eyes of hers certainly are sparkling now, Josh thought, taking in her delight. His patrons would eat her up, taking in her long tawny-reddish hair, her dazzling smile and the fluidity of her hands as she spoke.

"I know I do good work," Piper began. "And I'm so pleased you want my work. Do you buy the work outright or is it a commission setup? Would my work be scattered around or..." her voice faded.

"Primarily, your work will be showcased in its own room. I should like a few smaller pieces scattered about where they will echo and reflect the feel of various other rooms. I also have an idea about a focal piece, but I'll get to that in a moment. We usually work on a commission basis. The Gallery will pay you twenty-five percent of each sale."

"Twenty-f-five percent," her voice sputtered in her outrage. Color rose high on her cheeks. "Not less than sixty! I am the one who creates this 'evocative work, after all!"

"Thirty is pushing the limits for me," Josh responded, casually running an index finger along the sinuous sweep of a fire-red arc.

Her eyes shot daggers at him. "Fifty. Surely a 'visceral' reaction is worth that!"

"Forty," Josh replied, looking her straight in her eyes. "I have the Gallery, the contacts, the reach. I supply the advertising that brings people in and lets them see your work. I have the place to showcase your work far better than you can here. Forty," he repeated.

"Done," she said, putting out her hand to shake, happily trying to hide her excitement at getting a full five percent more than she'd anticipated.

"Done," answered Josh, noticing the flash in her eyes and getting exactly the percentage he wanted in the first place.

"Before we put anything to paper," Piper began, "please do

not EVER ask me for little unicorns with golden horns."

Horrified at the idea, Josh shuddered. "You will not have to worry about that. Any other concerns?"

"I create what I create. I don't do too well with 'art on demand' so to speak. I don't like being asked to do another 'exactly' like whatever. This is a war, of sorts. The glass and I battle it out to bring my ideas to life. No two pieces can ever, will ever be exactly the same. Even if I could, I wouldn't be happy with the result."

"No problem. Now I have a request for you. Without giving you parameters per se, I'd like you to come over to The Gallery today and look at a particular space I'd like to see your work showcased in. You really need to see it to get an idea of size, color, shape and form. I am 'thinking' a chandelier sort of thing, as it will be hanging, but, well, you'd need to see the space. Do you have time now? While you are doing that, I'll get the necessary paperwork prepared."

Forty-five minutes later, after Joshua had wandered around her studio getting more excited by the minute, they were standing in the two-storied atrium of The Gallery. Curved windows let the light flood in. She wandered, pondered, considered. She'd already briefly taken a tour of what she already thought of as 'her' area and seen the other artists' works in place in the other rooms.

"I really like the fact that you have the poetry scattered throughout the rooms," Piper said when Josh rejoined her. "I like the juxtaposition of words and art. Neither overshadows the other, or defines it, but rather enhances the possibilities, the experience."

He smiled. "So, any ideas about the possibilities of the atrium piece?"

"Hmm. Is this a piece you are planning to keep as a permanent installation or something that will be for sale?"

"My first thought is that it would be for sale thus allowing, over time, a variety of pieces being showcased in such a fashion."

"Okay then," she mused, craning her neck back and taking mental measurements. "I have a couple of ideas. One would be more a reflection of the concepts behind some of the decisions you've made here. The other idea, well, I'm still thinking about it. When would you need this? Would you want it in time for the opening? It will be a huge piece and will take some time to install as well."

"If possible, I would like to have it in place. Would you have enough time?"

"If you are happy with the number of pieces I already have finished, then yes..." she chewed on her bottom lip as she thought, "I should be able to. The ideas are spinning. I really need to get back to my studio."

"I'll make the arrangements for packing and shipping the work we've agreed upon. May I come by the studio to see how it is going?"

She shook her head, smiling. "No. I'll let you know when it's finished. Will you have a professional installer there to hang the piece? I expect it will be quite heavy. You are sure the ceiling can support the weight, and there's electricity wired in?"

"Yes, all that was part of the remodel of The Gallery, as I knew I'd want something in that space."

"It does cry out for something," she smiled. "Have you seen the light poles with the changing LED lights?"

"Yes, I have. Are you thinking of incorporating one into the piece?"

"Quite possibly."

"We can work with that. Just let me know the model you need and we will have it here."

"Two weeks. I need to get to work. I will call you to give you updates. Please don't call me. Have your people come and pack the rest up today. I don't want you underfoot or sneaking in for a peek!"

"Yes, Ma'am," Josh grinned. "No, Ma'am."

Later, sitting with Emily and the kids out on the back deck, Josh seemed distracted.

"Did your meeting with the glass artist go well today?"

"Hmmm …what? Oh. Yes, it went very well, actually. Her work is amazing, Em."

"You seem like you're a million miles away, hon."

"I'm sorry. There's just something about her. I don't know if I've met her before or seen her somewhere or what. I just feel as if I should know her. It keeps hovering around the edge and I can't shake it. It is driving me crazy!"

"Why don't you ask her?"

"It may come to that. She just seems so familiar." Josh shook his head as if to clear it. "It's kind of like when I saw Jinn and then you and didn't know you were two different people. I mean you don't automatically expect someone to have a twin. It just doesn't enter the equation."

"Well, I'm sure you'll figure it out at some point," Emily said encouragingly. "Is she going to create something for the atrium?"

"Yes, she is. I've been informed, quite emphatically I might add, that she will, but that I can't see it until it is finished and ready to be installed. In fact, if she has her way about it, I wouldn't see it until it is in place. Like that'll happen!"

"I'm sure it will be fine, dear," Emily said thinking back to an earlier phone call she'd received from a certain glass artist asking her if just such a thing might be arranged. Emily knew that given Josh's response to her work in general that he would, indeed, love whatever it was she'd come up with. Emily absently rubbed her hand over the cat's head. *Yes, I might just see if I can help Piper surprise him.*

Chapter 7

Devon and Hemingway showed up at Piper's door with a bottle of wine and a box of tissues.

"Life sucks. Can we come in?"

Knowing there was nothing much one could do when presented with that opening line, Piper scrapped her plan for a long bath and her new book, opened the door and gestured him in.

"What's going on, Devon?"

"Byron left me to go to Costa Rica with some guy he met at the bar this week." Devon dropped the cat on the floor and collapsed onto the couch.

Byron? "Who's Byron? I thought you and Augusto were hanging out."

"No, darling. Augusto was so last week. Besides, he wasn't a reader and I cannot be expected, as a writer, to have a real relationship with anyone who doesn't appreciate the written word, now, can I? I met Byron at that corner bookshop, Pages, down the hill and we recognized our inner souls immediately. "I thought he was *the one.* He's tall, dark in a sardonic sort of way, had long hair and was so well read. He was perfection."

"But he took off for Costa Rica with someone else he'd just met," commented Piper.

"I know. It is so unfair," Devon sniffed. "I even put off writing the next chapters of my book to go to the museum with him, and I'm at the climax of the whole 'world's colliding' section. I don't do that for just anybody, you know. My work is important, in an epic fantasy sort of way. Then he goes out for a drink with his sister and next thing you know, he texts me. *Texts* me to say he's headed to some foreign country with the guy."

Piper dropped to the couch and gave Devon a hug. "He wasn't worthy of you. You can do much better than some male slut named Byron."

Devon nodded. "You are so right. See? I told you, Hemingway. I was right to come over here."

Hemingway continued licking her paw and ignoring the both of them as her tail swished back and forth.

Piper stood and went into the kitchen, opened the freezer and came back to the couch with a half-gallon container of cookie-dough ice cream and two spoons. "You don't need wine, Devon. This calls for ice cream. 'Cookie-dough Fantasy' with cashews, chocolate chunks and caramel," she read off the label.

Devon took a spoonful of ice cream and thoughtfully took in the combination of sugars guaranteed to produce a sugar high, if not an emotional one.

"Yes. This does call for ice cream. I am so glad you moved in, Piper." Devon smiled. Then he wailed. "But I miss him."

"You should focus on your book, Dev. It's way more important than some idiot named Byron who didn't have the sense God gave a flea."

"I should." He stood up. "Can you watch Hemingway for a bit? She always tries to sleep on the keyboard when I'm upset. Oh, and can I take this with me?"

Piper waved him and the ice cream out the door and then stood there looking at the cat who was now sprawled regally on her coffee table, shedding with every purr.

She shrugged and decided that a bath was sounding even

better than it had earlier. Taking a glass and Devon's forgotten bottle of wine, she headed toward the tub.

She'd no sooner settled in and had her first swigs of the truly atrocious wine he'd brought when inspiration hit.

Words. Punctuation. Inflection. Writing. She could see the completed hanging sculpture. Still in black and white as she often first saw her work, she saw the exclamation points, semi-colons, and question marks suspended in a spiral interspersed with the globes of periods. She could see, not words themselves, but the varying squiggles and curly-cues of shorthand and maybe a few of those marks editors used for corrections. Those would need to be in red, she thought. Dark, dark blues, or perhaps, greys. Pops of color and clear glass balls of all sizes in-between.

'Possibilities' maybe? 'Book of Glass' or no, wait. 'From A Gathering of Glass.' Perfect! Words arranged 'just so' made up a book or poem. But, words picked from all the possible ones and fit together precisely to create something new and different … All *her* work, meanwhile, started with a gathering, a glob of molten glass, that with breath, moisture, gravity, and inspiration became whatever she would create. Plunged again and again into the fire, each time it became something new, something *more.*

Art, books, music, they all were like that. They started with a gathering of thoughts, ideas, impulses and became a new thing. The revision, editing, refining, movement, life itself all became a part of the whole.

People were even like that, she mused. *Wasn't she? Hadn't she been a gathering of glass that she'd molded and formed and reformed into who she was now? Hadn't she come through the fire of life and evolved?*

The Gallery itself, the people within it, had changed, been re-imagined in myriad ways. They and The Gallery too had faced the fire and not only survived, but were thriving.

Piper hopped out of the tub, tossed on her work clothes, grabbed her purse and the cat and headed out, stopping only to bang on Devon's door.

"Hi. Here's your cat. I gotta go to my studio. I need to work."

She whirled around and headed down the stairs. Devon stood there, bemused, scratching Hemingway under the chin. Then he went back to his writing. Hemingway, having been dumped on the couch, licked a paw, turned around three times and promptly went to sleep to the sound of keyboard clacking.

Chapter 8

Phee shook her head. What was with all the doors slamming and people clumping up and down the stairs at this hour of night? Didn't people know that some other people needed their sleep? Not that she was asleep anyway, but still ... Who could sleep with all the 'stuff' she'd dredged up from her visit to the shrink a few days ago? Then the papers arriving today from the court...

It was so unfair. Now her ex was saying that her being trans-gender was all in her head, that she was crazy, had some sort of mixed-up bi-polar thing going on. CIS women didn't get it. At all. In fact most people didn't. "It isn't that I *want* to be a woman, it is knowing I *am* a woman," she groused. "That's a huge difference."

Tears swam as she stomped around her apartment. "And now to be summarily informed that 'pending further investigation' that I'm not allowed to see Chloe? She's my daughter, for god's sake!"

Phee flopped into the overstuffed couch. *How can I fight this? I don't have money for more lawyers. What am I going to do? Bitch got almost every dime I'd had in the divorce. She knew how I felt. 'It's okay, baby, we can make it work.' Make it work, my ass!*

Now she was stuck, alone (as usual) with all these thoughts ramming around in her brain.

She didn't like it when her head had multiple Ping-Pong

games going on with thoughts bouncing every-which-way. Made it damn near impossible to focus on any one of them; not that they were such stellar thoughts to begin with!

I can't wait until I get finished with the damn counseling to be approved to get my ID changed and have my surgery. Such a pain. Here I am, twenty-four, plenty old enough to buy a damned bottle of Bailey's, and I get carded at check-out. I didn't want to dig out my card and have to explain and all that. So tiresome. Such a total drag. She left without the Bailey's. Not worth it. And, damn it, she wanted a drink!

Phee'd spent the day on one go-see opportunity after another go-see that her agent had sent her to check out. She'd only landed one. Timiny, down near the Bay, designed clothes that were exactly her style – vintage lace and very Victorian or Edwardian... every one of them. She'd have killed to wear his clothes, let alone own some. And he was known to be generous in that department. He liked his models wearing his clothes even when they weren't on a shoot. It was the only high point of the day.

Then there'd been the catalog go-see. *Catalog. Should have been an easy gimmie, but no. She wasn't 'their style.' They wanted whimsical and winsome. I can do winsome,* she thought, pouting winsomely.

Maybe she should dye her hair blond. No, she hated being blond and the root jobs were a killer.

She didn't know why Edwardo had even sent her on the next to last go-see. Swimsuits. Seriously? She couldn't do them yet. Soon, she hoped, if she ever could get the money up for the surgery. And then, adding insult to injury, the last one, at Gambio's, was basically for menswear! Their show was for male inspired women's suits. Ties and spats for god's sake! Damn if she would. As if! Not.

But she needed to land some more jobs fast or she'd be back to looking for sludge work. Why didn't people understand? No way could she handle transition and going to college full time, although she'd like doing that. Didn't know what, but she had to find something. Anything. She detested being a waitress. Pretty much sucked at it too. She wasn't stupid. She was more than willing to work hard. She was dedicated. "I am woman," she groused. "Hear me roar!"

Sure. Even to her, it came out as a whimper. Maybe tomorrow would be better. She had a couple of appointments set as well as another session with the shrink. Too bad he couldn't help her, but the word was you had to be all super-confident seeing them or they'd never hand out that golden ticket. She'd pretty much learned that with the last one. She was so glad he'd moved his practice. He gave her the creeps. It wasn't that he did anything out of line, but it was just the way he looked at her, like she was beneath him or something. How could she go and act as if she didn't have a care in the world? She couldn't. "Chloe," she wailed. How can I not see my kid? I need to see her. It's killing me not to see her every day, but not to see her at all? I am not crazy. I'm stuck in this body that isn't mine. How can they keep me from seeing her? It's just wrong. Everything's wrong. This really sucks.

Chapter 9

Emily listened for a moment and then went looking for six-and-a-half-year-old Emma. Alice and Journey, she knew, were with their dad on a quick trip to the store. She found Emma in her bedroom, sitting on her bed with Sherry curled up in her lap.

"Were you talking to the cat, Emma?"

"No, silly," she giggled. "I was talking to Auntie Jinn," replied Emma.

"Sweetie, you know your 'Auntie Jinn' is dead. Remember, we talked about that when you saw the pictures of her in the photograph album. She died before you were born."

"I know, Mommy, but she was here and we were talking about how my middle name and her name are the same. She really likes that I have both her names."

Emily shook her head. "Were you playing pretend again, Emmy?"

"No, Mommy. She sat here with me and I could hear her. She looked kinda funny, sorta see through, but she was here. I like her, Mommy. She's nice."

"Nice, well, she would be, of course. Is this the first time you've 'talked' to her?"

Emma laughed. "No, I see her lots. Ally can't see her though.

Auntie Jinn said that she might one of these days. But since Alice couldn't see her anyway, she comes now when it's just me. She likes The Gallery. She says she likes seeing Daddy's paintings."

"She does. Well then, right now it's time to get ready for bed. I hear Daddy and your sisters downstairs. See if you can get in your jammies before Alice comes upstairs, okay?"

"Okay, Mommy." Emma ran to her dresser and got her princess nightgown out of the drawer. "I'm going to be 'Princess Emma' tonight."

"You are always Princess Emma," smiled her mother as she headed downstairs to corral the other two children.

Later, after the kids were all sound asleep, Emily and Josh sat in the living room.

"Josh, I need to talk to you about something Emma told me this evening. She talks to Jinn."

"Pretends to, you mean."

"No, she's pretty insistent that they have entire conversations. She said that Jinn likes your paintings being in The Gallery and that she likes that Emma has both Jinn's names."

"Was she upset or scared?"

"No. She's quite happy and didn't seem the least bit upset about it. She likes talking to her and says that Alice can't see her. Yet."

"Maybe the move has her feeling a little unsettled and she's using an imaginary Jinn to make her feel better?"

"I don't know. It worries me. She seemed so matter of fact about it. I heard her talking and it sounded like she was having a conversation, although I couldn't hear her well enough to hear what she was saying. But I didn't hear the 'other' side of the conversation. If she were pretending, wouldn't she have pretended the rest of the conversation like she does with her dolls?"

"I don't know, babe. But as long as it doesn't seem to be something that is upsetting her, maybe we should just go along with it for right now."

"Maybe," Emily answered. "It just seems weird. I'm not sure what to do or say about it to her. I reminded her that Auntie Jinn died before she was born, but it didn't faze her in the slightest. She was very accepting that she could talk to her."

"You know what they say, about how when something doesn't make sense, then the logical thing is that she's telling you the truth, as strange as that might seem. You once told me that the dreams you had with Jinn in them seemed very real to you."

"That was a long time ago. Why would Jinn talk to Emma and not me?"

"Ah." Josh wrapped his arms around Emily in a hug. "That *would* bother you. I don't know, sweetheart. Maybe we'll just have to wait and see what happens. It's no stranger than our seeing Minami now, is it?"

"I suppose not," she smiled. "I hadn't thought of it like that. You're right."

"I wonder why now," Josh mused. "Minami came when we were both considering committing suicide. We are both long past that. The girls are fine; we are fine. If there's that sort of a connection. I don't know."

"Me neither, hon. Me neither. Oh. Total subject change. I received an email today from Peter McAllister, the art critic. You know, the one from that art book I've been dragging around with me forever? He's committed to being at the grand opening for The Gallery."

"Isn't that the same last name as your glass artist? I wonder if they are related."

"I don't think so. He had a son thirty years ago or so, but I've never heard mention of a daughter."

"Just coincidence then, I suppose. He'd have mentioned it, I guess."

"He doesn't really know who's being featured, at any rate. He does know about the Maidu pieces, and I mentioned C.M. Baker, but I'm keeping quiet about Piper's work until the opening. I think she'll make more of a splash that way."

"Did you ever figure out where you know her from or who she reminds you of?"

He shook his head. "No, I didn't. Even when I was at her studio, I kept feeling that I should 'know' her. She certainly didn't act as if she knew me at all," he shrugged. "She should have the atrium sculpture finished soon. We decided to have clear glass rods with LED lights in them coming down from a circular base in the ceiling. The base has been installed, along with the framework for the piece. I can't wait until she has it delivered and we get it in place."

Emily smiled. "You are so excited about it. I am too. It will make quite a statement. I bet it is going to look amazing from both inside and from the outside through those windows."

"I really like the way that so many of the pieces like C.M. Baker's 'Thevri' are viewable from two sides. It is all coming together," he finished with a smile.

"It sure is. And you, m'love are going to look so handsome in a tux!"

"I don't know why I ever agreed to making this a black tie affair. Of course, that means I get to see you in a long gown, so there is that," he smiled. "We've had some really long days, of late. Let's head upstairs."

Together, they headed upstairs, never noticing Jinn wafting through the room behind them.

Chapter 10

Phee settled in at the doctor's office for her next counseling session.

"Reviewing my notes from our last session, I get the impression that having the surgery will be very important to you. What will you do if it is a long time before you can actually afford the surgery?"

Phee shook her head. "It *is* very important to me. I need to feel like I'm not being forced to wear a mask any more. I want to be myself. As one of the few transgender models, it is excruciating to have to turn down possible gigs because I can't truly wear a swimsuit yet or because I need a different dressing room. Life will just be so much simpler after the surgery."

"Yes, on a lot of levels, it will be simpler. Yet, you do realize that all the problems won't vanish, don't you? Life is rarely simple. There are always little things mucking it up. It says here in your pre-counseling bio that you have a daughter. Is that causing any problems for you?"

Phee shuddered. She wasn't ready to talk about this with him. "Do we really need to talk about Chloe now?"

"Yes, I believe we do."

She sighed. "Yes, it is causing major issues. My ex managed to get the courts to keep me from seeing my daughter pending 'further investigation.'

"This is very common, Phee."

"Well, it shouldn't be," she exclaimed.

"While the courts are becoming more aware of transgender issues, they are still overly cautious (some might say) in these matters. Their "further investigation" is a fancy way of saying that they will wait until the counseling is almost complete before making a final ruling. At some point in time, with your permission, I will be called into the court to render my decision on how well you are handling the transition and explain my own feeling about your abilities to parent a child. Frankly," he continued, "I have yet to counsel a transgender individual of either sex who would *not* be an acceptable parent. Some need a bit more guidance than others, but in the end, the no contact order usually is rescinded. You just need to be patient with the process."

"It's hard. I am missing so much."

"I realize that. Perhaps you need to consider your priorities. Is seeing your daughter more important to you than your transition?"

"It is equally important. I should not have to choose."

"Well, at least Chloe is still very young. She will not remember much of this time in her life, if any. Once you finish your counseling, I am sure you will be able to fit back into her life. Frankly, it is far harder on you, at the moment, than it is on her."

"I suppose it is. I just wish everything was done. Counseling, the surgery, figuring out how to pay for it all, everything.

"I want to live my life and not feel like I'm the little kid peering through the toy store window at all the toys I can't have. I don't want to be on the outside of that window. I want to be where I can have and do and be who I am. It is so difficult to explain that to people. If they aren't on this side of the window, they simply cannot understand how thick that glass is, how big a deal it is to break through it. They live their lives, go after what's important to them. They don't need to transform; they *are*. I am so tired of being on the outside looking in."

"I understand. Phee, before we meet next time, I want you to start a journal. I want you to write down these thoughts, any thoughts you have as you go through this process. It may help you to see things more clearly, help you put things in perspective and give you a place to just ramble out your frustrations." He stood. I will see you in two weeks, I think. You are really doing very well and should be proud of yourself! In two weeks then."

Chapter 11

For days now Piper had been working on the piece for the atrium. Seventy-five glass balls, twenty three different squiggles for all the correctional markings and all the punctuation marks were complete. Now she needed to figure out what the words would be in shorthand and if they were something she could complete with blown glass. She was meeting with Emily tomorrow to get both the poem and the transcription into shorthand. She liked that the piece would incorporate something that was very special to both Josh and Emily but that could appeal to most anyone, should the piece be sold. Then again, perhaps no one but she, Josh and Emily would ever know that connection. Of course, Emily had made some noises that The Gallery would buy the piece outright. When it was done, it would be quite a surprise for Josh, she mused.

All of her other pieces had been delivered, and Piper was thrilled with the way Josh had chosen to highlight each one. She wasn't exactly thrilled to have to go buy a long gown for the opening, though. It would be her first formal event. Maybe Devon would have some ideas about what to wear. She certainly didn't by herself. She hadn't been in the area long enough even to know where to shop! The opening was only a couple of days away now;

she didn't have much time. Had to get this done first though. Shoes. She'd probably need new shoes too. Well, that wouldn't be all bad!

Meeting in the coffee shop around the corner from The Gallery, Piper sat with Emily reading the poem she'd written for the atrium piece. She'd done an excellent job, Piper thought, of meshing the blown glass images with both art and writing. She found it something of a coincidence that their thoughts ran so really parallel; Piper's original inspiration was very like the thoughts Emily expressed in writing. Looking at the shorthand transcription, she thought that she'd be able to recreate it in glass. Some figures leant themselves easily to a glass representation, and other words would take a bit of finagling, but that was the kind of challenge she liked. She was excited about it.

Emily was getting a charge out of Piper's use of shorthand in the piece.

"We use verbal shorthand all the time, in a sense, even though we don't tend to think of it that way."

"Body language is a form of it too, don't you think," said Piper, alerting the server they were ready to order by a simple movement of eyes and her head.

"Yes, it is. I am so glad we arranged to surprise him with having the piece installed first and then letting him see it. I really appreciate your working with me on this."

"Well, it'll be your job to keep him out of the way," laughed Piper. "I don't envy you that. He is very insistent on being involved every step of the way."

"Yes, he is. Normally, no one sets things up but him. I don't know how you've managed to keep him away from your studio all this time!" Emily shook her head in wonder.

"I told him if he gets underfoot, it won't be done in time. That scared him enough to leave me alone. It is very satisfying at the same time to realize that he trusts my skill in my craft to let me do this without a lot of interference, so to speak. Many times for commissioned pieces, I have to go back and forth to be sure colors are exactly right, that the translucence is perfect, that this, that or the other thing is the way the people who've ordered it want it. I like that he's letting the piece evolve. I absolutely know he will be pleasantly surprised."

"Yes. He's going to love it," Emily assured Piper. "I am equally sure that he will want to have it be a permanent display in The Gallery."

"I am working on another piece as well. Josh told me about the journey the two of you took to Jukai."

Emily looked surprised. Josh didn't usually talk about Jukai to anyone other than her.

"Really?"

"You seem surprised, and I do understand that. The piece I'm working on is a smaller piece that will, I expect, end up near the painting he did of the ribbons in the forest. It is a tangle of red, yellow and blue ribboned swirls of glass. I am calling it 'Destinations.' The yellow and red swirls are sort of knotted together near the heart of it. I'm really pleased with how it is turning out. It'll be finished before the opening too."

"Ribbons have become rather special to us. I can't wait to see it!"

"Now, Emily – you have figured out how to keep him away from the gallery Friday, right? It will take about four hours to get it all hung."

"Yes, despite all the last minute details we have to take care of before Saturday, I am dragging the kids and him off to San Francisco for the day. You should have a good six hours to your-self. Text me if you need more time, and I'll be sure to side-track him somehow. Do leave the lights on when you're finished. Or do you want to be there when we arrive?"

"I'd love to be in on the surprise. Thank you for thinking of that," Piper smiled. "Text me when you're close. You said there'd be people there to help?"

"Yes, and they will begin building the scaffolding as soon as we leave. It should all go quite smoothly. He is going to be so surprised!"

"Yes. I'd best take the poem and head to my studio when we finish our coffee. You do have another copy of it?"

"Yes, and now that you've approved it, I'll get it printed, matted and framed. I figured on going with a black mat and frame and the guys know where I want it hung. So we are all set with that.

"Have you picked out what you are wearing Saturday?" Emily asked.

"Not yet," Piper said. "Haven't been to a black tie event in ages! Guess I will have to schedule some shopping time in."

"Me too," grimaced Emily. "But it'll be worth it, seeing Josh in a tux!"

"Do you mind if I have an escort for the night? I know Saturday is by invitation only."

"Of course not," Emily smiled. "Besides, I expect you will be there before it starts, so it won't be an issue. In the meantime, I will look forward to seeing you Friday night when we get back!"

Chapter 12

"Mommy says you're dead," Emma said, looking up at Jinn.

"I am. Does that scare you?" Jinn wafted around so that she was facing Emma.

"No. Should it?"

"Not in this case. I neither could nor would hurt you or your family. Ever."

"If you are dead, are you a ghost?"

"I suppose."

"I thought there was no such thing as ghosts."

"Ah. There's a lot that the living do not understand."

"Where are you when you're not here? Mommy said you were in Heaven."

"Your mother is very wise," Jinn replied without answering the question. "She is a very good mother to you and your sisters. She is happy now."

"You don't look happy."

"But I'm not sad either. I am… waiting, I suppose."

"For what? I don't like waiting for things."

"Neither do I, little one, but what can you do? You can't hurry everything up or you'd run out of time, it would all puddle together and you wouldn't be able to anticipate the good things, the fun things to come."

"Why are you here?"

"To help someone."

"I like helping Mommy."

"I bet you do."

"Are you going to help someone get to Heaven? Are you an angel?" Emma was full of questions.

"No, I'm no angel and no, I hope not to help someone get to heaven. I hope to show them how to live."

"Oh. Mommy thinks I'm making you up. You should let Mommy see you, then she'll know you aren't pretend."

"I will, in time. When she's ready."

"More waiting."

Jinn smiled. "Yes, more waiting."

"If I wait long enough, do you think maybe I'll ever get a grandma? My friend Missy has one. She makes cookies. Mommy says we don't have any, because our grandmas are all in Heaven."

"Would you like a grandmother or a grandfather?"

"I don't know any grandfathers. Are they nice like Missy's grandma?"

"Of course they are," Jinn told her.

"Then yes, I would like one. Missy doesn't have a grandfather, just two grandmothers."

"Maybe you will have a grandfather then," smiled Jinn. "You never know what the future might bring. You really should go to sleep. I will see you again soon. Sleep now. Sleep."

Emma's eyes dropped, she rolled over and snuggled in with her doll.

Jinn smiled, looked around almost sadly, and drifted off through the wall.

Chapter 13

Piper finished up the last of the shorthand pieces for the atrium sculpture and put them in the annealing oven.

She took one of the red glass rods and heated it in the glass oven. Resting the rod in the steel base, she took her tweezers and pulled the end of the glass, stretching it and then curling it. Using the shears to cut the glass, she heated a pontil and attached it to the end of the glass rod. Walking back to the oven, she reheated it, spinning, spinning, always spinning, fighting gravity and using gravity to maintain the desired shape. Again, using her tweezers, she pulled some more, curling the glass around a thick steel rod and then removing the rod to leave a long, gently twisted spiral.

Over at the table in front of the annealing oven, she heated the glass where it was attached to the pontil and then, using her crimper in one hand and supporting the rest of the long, ribboned curl on an insulated mitt with the other, she worked the crimper around the end to crimp the edge. Dropping the tool in its slot, she picked up a short rod and smartly tapped it on the glass. The glass fell away from the pontil and lay on the mat. Heating a paddle with the blow torch, she gently smoothed the end of the ribbon before placing it on another insulated mat.

Twice more, she repeated the process, using rods of blue and yellow. Each had been twisted in such a way that once complete, she could fit them together, loosely spiraled around each other. The third wove around the first two and then went off in a different direction from the others. The red and yellow ribbons began separately at the base, but then curled around and became one at the top.

Attaching the sculpture to the pontil, she warmed it, spinning, spinning it, letting the heat and fire add its own dimension. Smiling, Piper crimped the end, rapped it and the completed sculpture rested on the mitt. Carefully placing it in the annealing oven, she set the timer for in the morning.

Swiping her forearm across her forehead and shrugging her shoulders to work out the knotted kinks, she reached in the small fridge for a bottle of water. Noticing the hour, she grimaced. The ribbons had taken over three hours for her to get them exactly right. Twice she'd started over, working the vision, fighting the glass, but she'd done it. She could see it in the gallery now, rising from a bed of satin ribbons.

She needed to get home, shower and change. She had shopping to do. She needed to find an evening gown for the Grand Opening.

Showered, dressed, wearing her new lace bra and panties under her dress and feeling delightfully feminine, which, as any girl knows, is the only way to go out to find 'the dress,' she was finishing up a glass of juice when there was a knock on the door. Devon popped through it.

"Oh my, don't we look exquisite tonight. And where are we off to?"

"Shopping, of all things." She considered Devon a moment. "Devon, darling, do you own a tux?"

He looked at her with an expression somewhere between shocked and puzzled. "I do. Might I ask why?"

"Because you, owner of the magnificent Hemingway Houdini across the hall, will have the honor of escorting me to the grand opening at The Gallery Saturday evening."

"Really. *Moi, Cherie?* I should be delighted to be included in such a high-brow affair and, m'dear, to witness the glorious success you shall have."

"The Gallery's success, Devon." She smiled. "Of course, hopefully, my work will be well received as well. It is my first show since returning to the states," she said preening.

Devon made a noncommittal sound. "Where shall we go to find you the perfect dress?"

"We?"

"I love you to pieces, darling, but you do, if you don't mind my saying so, need a bit of help in the 'divine garment' department."

"You'd go shopping with me?" Piper said in some wonder. "I thought guys hated shopping. Especially for clothes."

"Straight guys, maybe, but those of us who know better absolutely love it. And we love nothing better than taking on a neophyte and showing her the ropes. I am amazed that you didn't return from abroad with at least three statement gowns. Everyone does, you know. Seriously darlin', you'd think you hadn't been shopping for clothes in your whole life."

Piper cracked up laughing. "Oh Devon, remind me sometime to tell you a story about my time 'abroad.' Oh my, too, too funny."

"Tell me now, you know how I love a good story!"

"We haven't the time. Gown shopping, remember?"

"Right. Let me think," said Devon. "It's past September. Winter white? No, not with your hair, your skin. How are your shoulders? D'ya have good shoulders? I know you have boobs there somewhere...cleavage or no? Hmm."

Piper just stared at him. Maybe this wasn't such a good idea. This was hard enough on her own. She still wasn't really comfortable clothes shopping.

"Green. With your glorious red hair all swept up in one of those loosely curled and 'artfully careless' dos," Devon continued turning her around. "Deep, deep green, long sleeved, long gown, off the shoulder, deeply plunging and gathered with some sort of glass brooch. You can make that tomorrow, can you not?"

"I ... uh ... sure, I think."

A knock and then Phee's head peeked in. "Did I hear long, green gown?"

"Yes, you did. I'm about to take our resident star out to get her clothes for the big show at the Gallery on Saturday."

"What size are you?" Phee asked Piper.

"Ah, a six or seven depending."

"Oh. Too bad. I'm a four on a bad day. Well, take her to Timiny's," Phee said decisively. "She'd look fabulous in his clothes. Ask for Claryce, she's the best fitter there. Make sure they know it is for the opening. You should get a discount." Waving goodbye to Phee, who'd been dying to be asked along but wasn't, Devon and Piper headed out to Timiny's.

Piper watched uneasily as Devon and the aforementioned Claryce consulted together, using much hand movement, rolled eyes and laughter. Claryce vanished and Devon walked back to Piper.

"She says she has exactly the thing," he said excitedly.

"The thing?"

"The dress, you silly girl. Ah, here she comes. Go. Go try it on. You will look divine in it, I can tell already."

Although Claryce offered to help her into the gown, Piper all but shoved the eager girl out of the dressing room.

I love being a girl, but I must be the only one on the planet that doesn't go ga-ga over getting this dressed up, she muttered to herself.

Almost exactly as Devon had described earlier, it was a deep hunter green with a gathering (how apt, she thought) where the material came together at the base of a deeply plunging neckline.

Removing her lacy bra, she put the dress on over her head. It slid down over her hips, puddling a bit on the floor, but heels would take care of that.

"Darling, what size are your feet?" came Devon's voice over the opened top of the door. "Are you decent, I want to see!"

"Size eight and no, not yet," she replied looking at herself in the dreaded three-way mirror. She turned, looking at how the gown fell in rippling waves down the back. With her hair up, a curl or two cascading, she might look pretty damned decent after all.

"Here." A pair of shiny gold, sling back, four-inch heels appeared at the top of the door. "Put these on. And hurry. I want to see."

"Thanks. Wait," she replied. She sat, slipping the shoes on, to discover they fit perfectly. Taking a hair comb from her purse, she artfully coiled her hair up on top of her head and stuck the comb in to hold it up.

Piper smiled and opened the door.

Devon's jaw dropped. Claryce smiled. A girl just coming around the corner stopped in her tracks and gaped.

"Sheer perfection, Piper. Turn, turn. Ahh," Devon smiled. "You'll be the belle of the ball at The Gallery."

Piper blushed. *I'm actually blushing,* she thought. *Wow.*

"A round, flattened swirl of color, here," he patted the base of the V. "Ever made jewelry before?" At the shake of her head, he continued. "Just add a couple of large safety pins when the glass is still hot. You can do amazing things with safety pins."

"Um, excuse me? You look so beautiful. Did I hear you say you are going to the Grand Opening at The Gallery on Saturday?" A shopper stood in front of Piper, just staring. A diminutive blond with choppy hair, glasses and huge grey eyes, she continued, "I am, too. Least, I'm supposed to be. I hate openings, but I'm told I have to go since my work's there," she finished in a rush, looking miserable.

Piper almost felt bad for the clearly uncomfortable girl. "I'm Piper," she said. "My glasswork is being shown at The Gallery."

"You're PIPer?" she almost squeaked. "Oh wow, your work is

incredible! I saw it when I brought some more of my stuff in to Josh. I'm—"

"C.M. Baker!" finished Piper. "Your work is pretty amazing too! I love the way you actually are able to play with light and shadows."

"Well, isn't this just the mutual admiration society," interjected Devon.

"But this is the artist I was telling you about, Dev," Piper looked at Devon. "The one with the incredible trees."

"Ah," he smiled. "I see. She really has gone on about your work. So you're buying a dress here too?"

"I might. I need something, but…" her voice trailed off miserably, clearly ill at ease next to the svelte figure of Piper.

"Claryce! We need you, darling. We need a fabulous dress for this dear, dear friend of ours. She too, is one of the featured artists at the Grand Opening at The Gallery," he said meaningfully, giving her a sharp look.

"Hmm. Okay. I can work with this." Claryce looked at C.M. Baker, had her turn. "Hmm. Good skin, lovely golden undertones. Do you have someone who can do your make-up? You need a special touch with glasses, you know."

"Ah…"

"Yes, she does," fussed Devon. "I know just the gal who will do both your make-ups and hair. Special evening and all. You both must dazzle!"

"I don't do 'dazzle,'" muttered C.M.

"You will on Saturday, m'dear. You will on Saturday!"

Claryce returned and bustled C.M. off to a dressing room.

"You do look spectacular, Piper. We must find you some earrings to match the gown, and a clutch, of course. If you don't have something, I expect Phee will. She has three times too much of everything. I swear, sometimes, it is like she overcompensates, but only God knows for what," he laughed.

C.M. came hesitantly out of the dressing room just as Piper

was about to return to hers.

She had on a long, flowing bronze column that slimmed her down and made her look almost pagan.

"You look like the conquering warrior, darling," enthused Devon. "Claryce, you are a treasure, an absolute gem. This is the perfect dress, in the perfect color for her. Look at yourself, C.M! You look wonderful!"

C.M. turned, and grinned. "I do. I really do."

"You must have my friend Rondar add some bronze highlights to your hair and he'll do green with a touch of bronze for your eyes. The dress makes your skin positively glow!"

Claryce returned from wherever she'd vanished. "Excuse me, folks. I'd like to introduce you to Timiny. He is the one who designed both your gowns."

"How beautiful you ladies are," Timiny smiled. "I understand that you are both artists who are showing at The Gallery. That is the opening for the entire season, I hear! Everyone will be there."

"I think I feel sick," murmured C.M.

"Suck it up, sweetheart, get used to being a star," said Devon, elbowing her before turning to Timiny. "Yes, these are two of the featured headliners."

"Then I insist you just take these gowns. They are on me. Do, of course, be sure to tell anyone who asks you what you are wearing that you are wearing Timiny from his new fall line. You will do that, won't you?"

C.M. Baker's eyes grew even larger. "Of course, we will," she responded.

"Well, I must be off, places to go, people to meet. Enjoy, enjoy." And with that Timiny swished out, leaving the girls silent and Devon ginning like the Cheshire cat.

"Well, didn't you both just score!"

"Free?" squeaked C.M. Baker, realizing what had just happened.

"Whew!" gasped Piper. I expect we both would have had

to sell everything to pay for these gowns. But aren't they just divine?!"

C.M. smiled. "I've never had a gown like this," she said excitedly, as Claryce returned with dress bags for the women.

"Okay, my darlings. Both of you need to be at Rondar's 'round the corner – no later than noon. You will both be there, right?"

C.M. nodded. So did Piper.

"Good! With what you didn't spend tonight, you can get the works at Rondar's.

Feeling mightily pleased with himself, Devon swept them both out the door.

Chapter 14

Early the next morning, Piper, still on something of a giddy high from the previous evening, made a gather of clear glass. Gently spinning the pipe, she puffed air into the pipette to make a small glass ball. Putting it back into the oven for a moment, she removed it and rolled the ball into some green fletz before she put it back into the fire. When the green was melted, she blew and made the ball slightly bigger before swirling it onto some reds and blues.

Spinning the pipe quickly this time as it yet again heated in the oven, she spun and spun until, using a paddle, she flattened the ball onto itself. She crimped it off and let it land on the mat when it fell. Then, as it lay, using a torch she heated the middle of it. Laughing, she used her tweezers to place two large safety pins in the center of the piece, placing them more or less near the top and bottom edges. Holding the pins in place as the glass hardened, she put it in the annealing oven. At the same time, she removed the last of the ribbon pieces from the annealing oven and put them on the table to box them up. Then she pulled the last of the shorthand pieces from the oven and packed them as well, one by one. Putting all the boxes in her car, she returned to get the rest of the materials and tools she'd need and headed over to the gallery.

The long clear tubes with the LED lights had been installed and they hung in a circle from the ceiling of the atrium. Outside of the light base were two concentric black metal circles with holes in them that would be used to insert the hooks that, in turn, would hold up individual pieces of glass. The outer circle was four and a half feet in diameter. The inner circle was just a yard across. The scaffolding was in place and there were several men milling around to help.

She'd premeasured each wire according to her diagram and was able to hand off the wired pieces to be hung in a semi-circular sequence. She'd decided only to use a few of the 'editorial' correction marks and stuck mostly with the punctuation marks and the 'short-hand' poem. Four feet wide, six feet long, the shorthand piece came together exactly as she'd envisioned.

After the men disassembled the scaffolding, she turned the switch and watched the LED lights as they bounced and reflected through the globes and twisted, curled glass. She couldn't wait to see how it would look at night, but she knew, just knew it would look perfect.

The men had hung the black framed and matted poem midway along the length of the stairway that encircled the atrium. Large enough to read easily, the flowing calligraphy enhanced the overall effect.

Piper then went to set up the ribbon piece on a green pedestal near Josh's painting of the ribbons in Jukai. She'd decided to name the piece 'Destinations' and had brought three spools of silken, half-inch ribbon to add to the display. Unraveling all three at the same time, she let them puddle on the stand. Then she set the sculpture dead center on top of the ribbon and let some of the ribbon lie back over the base of the sculpture itself.

Setting the small placard with the name of the piece in a three footed stand, Piper stepped away to view the result. Nodding, pleased with the overall effect, she collected her tools and headed back to her studio to retrieve the glass brooch she'd made earlier.

Emily texted Piper when they were about fifteen minutes away from The Gallery. Piper returned to meet them outside the building. The hanging sculpture in the atrium looked amazing in the gathering dusk, Piper thought as she waited for them to arrive.

When the family finally pulled up and started to walk toward the front entrance, Joshua stopped dead in his tracks, his gaze sweeping upward. He stared.

"It's up already. I thought we were... it was supposed to be..."

Emily pulled him to the door and unlocked it. "In," she said.

Josh led them in and looked and circled and smiled. He hadn't noticed the poem on the wall as yet, he was far too fascinated walking in circles under the piece.

"Piper, it is spectacular. Those are punctuation marks," he realized aloud. "The others, the swiggles and swoops..." he paused, "are they shorthand?" he asked incredulously.

Piper smiled and then pointed to the wall. Josh raced up the stairs to read.

Once formless
molten glass
we are gathered.
Blown by the winds of chance,
nurtured through water, air
we spin.
Gravity circles:
we expand our horizons
becoming more
as we evolve
into what
we are meant to be.

Emily VanAllen 2015

Josh grinned. "Emily, that is fantastic! The poem, the piece, it pulls in what we do, what Piper does, what this gallery is. Perfect!" He gathered both Piper and Emily into one large hug and spun them around. "Tomorrow is going to be the best day ever!"

"There is something else new for you to see, Josh," Emily said leading him to where the new piece waited on its stand.

"'Destinations'," read Josh, running his index finger softly along the swirl of 'ribbon,' pausing where the red and yellow ribbons contested.

"I knew you'd understand," Piper smiled. "It just seemed to fit here and with the two of you and your experiences. I saw to it that the other new pieces I created are all set as well. It's been a very busy week for me. I'll see you tomorrow. I am so glad you like the atrium piece."

"I think," said Joshua looking over to Emily, "that we must settle on a price for it. I really think it needs to be a permanent piece here."

"Next week will be soon enough. Besides, how many artists can claim a permanent piece of theirs on exhibit? We will work something out. Although, perhaps the rest of the world won't know about the deal you get," she grinned.

Josh made a motion of locking a key in front of his lips before handing the same imaginary key to Piper.

He and Emily walked Piper to the door and watched her get in her car and leave.

"I still can't figure out where or how I know her," Josh said. "It is such a strong feeling, a connection, almost. I wish I could figure it out."

"You will," said Emily linking her arm with his. "Now let's go get these kids fed and ready for bed, shall we? They've been very good and awfully quiet. Let's not push our luck!"

Outside, Josh and Emily chased the girls around to the back deck. With much giggling and laughter after what had been a day full of fun, everyone tumbled back into the house.

Chapter 15

Devon showed up at Phee's door around ten the next morning. He had left Hemingway behind this time, as there was just too much interesting and forbidden stuff for her to get into at Phee's. He arrived carrying just coffee and doughnuts instead.

Phee answered the door looking haggard, sleepy and just a bit off. Devon's mind clicked and answers spun into place, but his expression never changed as he came in chatty and full of the adventures of the night before. He told her all about their evening, thanked her for sending them to Timiny's and explained how nice Timiny had been about the gowns.

He asked her about her possibly having earrings and a clutch purse that Piper could borrow, which, of course, she did. Faux emerald earrings, a gold clutch and a cup of coffee later, and Phee was left alone again in the quiet.

Flopping onto her bed, she groused jealously to herself about gala events and big nights out. She couldn't remember the last big night out *she'd* had. *Life simply was not fair,* she thought. *Piper and Devon had even met C.M. Baker! C.M. was like the ghost of the art world in the area. Everyone knew her work, but few had ever met her or even knew if C.M. was a male or a female! Not that it mattered, of course, but still.* Phee rolled over, punching her pillow.

She was so lonely. So alone. Even though she'd done what she knew was right for her, going from a family atmosphere with a kid to being alone in an apartment was a huge change. She didn't like that part of the deal at all.

Going into the bathroom, Phee took her morning hormone pills and looked at herself in the mirror. *God, she was a wreck.* Her hair hung lank, she had shadows on her shadows. *I look like a freak of nature.* "You are, darling," she told herself. Hearing a knock at the door, Phee went back to see what Devon forgot to ask to borrow for Piper. Except, it wasn't Devon.

A County Sheriff stood there, holding an envelope in his hand. "Phoenix Lane?" he said, sounding terribly official.

"Yes," Phee answered hesitantly.

"I need you to sign for this, please, ah, ma'am."

"What is it?"

"I don't know. I'm just the delivery man."

"Oh. Well, okay." She signed and the officer left. Sitting at the kitchen table, Phee turned the envelope over and over in her hands. *Now what?* What else had her ex done to complicate her life? Finally, Phee ran her nail under the edge of the flap.

It was an eviction notice. Pay back rent within thirty days or she'd need to get out and quit the premises. What?

I'm not that far behind in rent, am I? I guess I must be. One more thing, she sighed. As if everything else wasn't enough. *Damn. Now what the hell was she supposed to do?*

She heard voices as people clumped down the stairs. From the snippets she heard, it sounded as if Piper was off for a spa day to get ready for her big night. *I want a spa day. Wish I could afford one of those.* Hearing Devon head back upstairs, she wondered if maybe he'd have a brilliant idea or three.

Phee got dressed, opting for hippy-chic with a tie-dyed skirt and lace camisole under a muslin blouse. She slipped on a pair of blue ankle boots and headed up to the third floor.

"Got a minute or two?" she asked Devon when he answered his door. Hemingway came out and wove her way between Phee's legs.

"Sure. C'mon in, please excuse the mess. Want some more coffee?"

She nodded, looking around for a place to sit. Books were piled everywhere! Catalogs were piled where the books weren't. Clothes were stacked haphazardly, some folded, most not. An odd green and blue sock hung from a lamp shade, coffee cups had grey sludge in the bottoms and the calendar was still on July.

Seeing her look around in barely masked dismay, Devon shrugged and said, "The cleaning woman took the last year off." Hemingway didn't seem to mind as she nudged a pile of t-shirts into a cozy nest, turned around three times and proceeded to lick the tip of her long tail. Devon handed Phee a cup of coffee and, in the same motion, grabbed a pile of jeans and dumped them on the floor to make a place for her to put the cup down again if she wanted to. He sat at his oversized desk.

For the next two hours and three cups of coffee, Devon sat, listened, offered tissues and listened some more. To his way of thinking, she didn't really seem to want any suggestions, but more, someone to listen to her extensive list of woes and misfortunes. He did offer some ideas, told her that, if she got some money to Stewie, the landlord would back off, and he mentioned that he knew of a few places that were hiring (even if he couldn't imag- ine her working at Home Depot or even Big Boy for that matter. She was a rather odd duck, after all).

Surreptitiously, he checked the time and knew he had to move her on her way. However real her problems were, he'd heard enough about the ex hating her guts for 'deciding' she was really a woman (she'd apparently assumed he'd known she was trans, though until this morning, he hadn't, exactly) and how she missed her kid, how expensive surgery was and how she couldn't get a gig modeling. He'd more or less tuned her out, thought about including a transgender character into his book, discarded that idea entirely and still managed to insert 'uh-huhs' and 'oh dears' into the appropriate pauses.

For some reason, she seemed to think he could wave a magic wand and make all her troubles disappear. *We all got issues, lady,* he thought to himself. *I could go on for hours about Byron or Arturo or being lonely. But the bottom line was, that in reality, no one really cared or gave a shit. That's why he wrote fiction. At least his characters had it good. Well, most of the time,* he conceded. *'Course, some of her shit might be usable for his Desmond character,* he mused. But for now, she needed to go back to her apartment so he could see if he could even find the tux he knew he had around here someplace or, heavens! He'd have to go out and rent one.

Pointedly looking at his watch, he stood. Phee rose to her feet as well and let him gently shove her out the door.

It only took him half an hour to find his tux shoved way in the back of the hall closet. He smiled, considered that he didn't need to shower for another three hours, sat at his desk and within moments was lost on the planet Altox and the epic battle between the indigenous Altoxicans and the invading hoard of Fremish.

Downstairs, Phee found a bottle of vodka she'd forgotten she had and poured herself a drink. Maybe, that would help. Devon and his mangy cat certainly hadn't.

Chapter 16

Josh and Emily had their hands full. With each of them on their phones handling details about the evening to come, the kids running around hyper with all the runoff excitement, calls beeping in on calls – it all was driving them both to distraction.

Emily, finally off the phone for a moment, handled the guy who had arrived holding a large, long box. "Josh, do we actually have a red carpet for tonight?" At his nod, she pointed the delivery man to the appropriate place to lay it out. No sooner had he left, her phone rang and it was KNTV followed minutes later with a call from KBCW.

"Josh, Josh!"

"Hold a moment, please," he said muting his phone. "I'm on a call with KTVU, make it quick."

"I just got off the phone with two other TV stations. They both will have cameras rolling!"

"Yeah, the last three calls were either from TV stations or the radio. It's going to be a lot bigger night than I thought! Oh, and I got a call from the governor's office. They wanted to know if there'd be a good time for the governor to stop by." He waved off any response from her. "Gotta get back to this."

Emily got up to answer a knock at the back door. "Oh, Beth.

You are here early!"

"I thought maybe it would be easier if I took the girls over to my place." Looking around, she added, "It looks like it's absolute chaos here."

"It is and yes, yes, yes, please! Girls, Miss Beth is here and she's taking you to her place."

Squeals erupted and all three girls ran to grab jammies, stuffed animals and whatever they needed for the night at Miss Beth's.

"Whatever they didn't grab, I'll have," assured Beth. "You know they have clothes at my place as well. Take some time, take a long bath and relax a little. It is going to be a long, exciting night. Have you eaten? Eat something," she commanded, handing her the bag she was carrying before Emily even had a chance to answer.

Herding the girls out the door and into her van, Beth waved and drove off. The ensuing silence was deafening.

"Hey," Josh walked in the door, "it's quiet."

"Beth came and snagged the girls to take them to her place for the night."

"Merciful woman, great idea! What's in the bag?" he said taking it from Emily. Opening it, he grinned and reached in to grab a tuna fish sandwich. "Food! Didn't realize how hungry I was," he said around a mouthful. "Eat one."

The phones stayed silent for a moment and they were both able to eat and have a cup of coffee.

Emily spoke around a mouthful of sandwich. "Oh, C.M. Baker is coming after all. Piper told me. Apparently they met getting gowns last night."

"Good," Josh said. "I was hoping she'd reconsider. Do you know, most folks haven't a clue whether she's a guy or a girl because no one's met her; they just know, have or want her work."

"It'll be good for all our exhibiters tonight that an art critic is coming tonight as well."

"Not just one. From the calls I've had today, every critic in the area will be here. This is it, babe. Major hit," he paused, "or epic fail."

"Hit, sweetie. We will absolutely be a hit. How can we not? Everything is ready, The Gallery looks amazing and the most handsome gallery owner in the world is on hand."

"Not to mention the most beautiful woman on the planet," he said sweeping her an exaggerated bow.

"Not dressed like this, I'm not," she giggled. "I need to head upstairs and begin my transformation from duck to swan."

"You could show up bald and wearing a flour sack and you'd put all the glamorous people to shame," he said gallantly.

"And really cause a scandal on the 11 o'clock news," she smirked. "Keep track of your time, even though it won't take you long to get ready. Your tux is all laid out in the bedroom. Everything you need is on the nightstand. Here, take my phone. I won't have a free hand."

Walking away as Emily headed upstairs, Josh already had one phone on hold while he talked into the other.

Jinn felt herself being tugged away from The Gallery and her sister. She settled on the railing of a second floor apartment balcony to wait to see what would happen.

PART Two : THE SCULPT

Chapter 17

Piper arrived back from Rondar's with her glorious red hair arranged in an upswept do, its curls artfully arranged to look careless. She'd been mani-ed and pedi-ed, made up and pampered and exfoliated to within an inch of her life. Her skin was glowing, her eyes were shining and she was totally relaxed – rather than being the bundle of nerves she had expected to be.

She'd had a lot of fun getting to know C.M. (who was now more 'Cee' rather than both separate initials) to the point that she'd even enlightened Cee about why this was such a big deal for her, above and beyond being a major showing. Cee didn't even hesitate. In fact, she was far more accepting than Piper could have imagined. She made one quick statement, and then they were both back to deciding polish colors and Cee's being flat out determined that Piper have the first pedi of her life.

They'd laughed, giggled, blushed and been pampered in tandem and enjoyed every second of it. They'd agreed that they both felt marvelous and energized when they'd parted ways, planning to meet up later at The Gallery.

Now all Piper had to do was relax for an hour or so, get dressed and head to The Gallery with Devon, who'd tagged her on her cell with the news that he'd sprung for a limo for the night.

'Champagne, darling. You don't want to have to worry about driving.'

Phee poked her head out her door as Piper hit the second landing. "Don't you look all beautiful? Love the hair, Cherie, do you have a bottle of something, anything to drink?"

Piper thought, nodded. "C'mon up and I'll give it to you."

Phee followed Piper up to the third floor and into her apartment. "I love what you've done with the place. Your gown is to die for! I must see you in it on your way out, okay? Oh, thank you, this will be great," she said taking the nearly full bottle of Jameson's that Piper offered to her.

"Well, I really appreciate your telling me about Timiny. My gown is so gorgeous."

"He's pure genius, no doubt. Gotta fly, thanks!"And Phee was gone down the stairs.

Shaking her head, Piper thought to herself that Phee already had been drinking a bit. Then she remembered the earrings Devon had borrowed for her and went over to hold them up in front of the mirror. They'd be perfect. Piper smiled. She had never felt quite so pretty in her life, and she wasn't even dressed yet.

She knew she wasn't as girly as some trans women were. She didn't feel the desire never to wear pants ever-ever again as many did. She understood the sentiment, absolutely, but it was different for her. Even as her outsides had once been a shell, albeit the 'wrong' shell, clothes were, to her, just a different sort of shell. It was what she was inside that really mattered. And now that her body matched the insides, she was complete and happy and could rock skinny jeans and boots with the best of them. When she even thought about it, that is. Funny, she mused, how the clothes weren't quite as important to her as they once were. She didn't feel as if she were making that outward statement she once did. She didn't need to anymore, she just *was*. She was good with that.

Yet, today was special and God knew she certainly felt special. She couldn't wait to get dressed, but knew she needed to wait an hour or so, else she'd be standing around afraid she'd spill something on her gown. Checking the time for the third time in less than five minutes, she giggled at herself. *You've all the time in the world. Enjoy the moment,* she told herself.

From downstairs, she could hear the music that Phee was playing. All by herself, with her arms around an imaginary partner, Piper waltzed around her apartment to the strains of "I Feel Pretty" from *West Side Story.*

When Devon knocked on her door (not simply bursting in as he now usually did) Piper was just putting on her lipstick. "Come in," she said just loudly enough that she knew he'd hear.

He opened the door, stopped in his tracks and positively goggled at her. Then fanning his hand in front of his face he said, "Darling, you are magnificent. The brooch you made is perfect! You look absolutely royal!"

"The safety pins were a great idea," she said, and then continued in the same quiet voice, "I have never, ever felt this way in my entire life. I feel as if I am beautiful!"

"That's only because you truly are, silly woman."

"Dev, you have no clue."

"So. What about me, darling? Do I pass muster enough to escort such a femme-fatale as yourself?" He spun in a circle.

"Aren't we the two headed off to the prom?" smiled Piper. "You are very handsome. What did Hemingway think?"

"I got her purr of approval," he chuckled. "Our chariot awaits, m'lady. Shall we go stun all the little people?"

Piper grabbed her wrap, and they started downstairs. She knocked on Phee's door as promised, and when Phee answered, she told her they were off and went through the 'You look awesome' routine. She and Devon promised to stop by when they returned if Phee's lights were on.

"If I don't answer, open the door, come in and holler. I'll be here. I want to hear all about it."

They promised and continued down to the limo.

"This is a night of firsts," Devon commented as they sat in the back seat looking at the flowers in small vases by the door, the full mini-bar and the rope lighting that lined the ceiling. "I've never been in a limo before."

"Me, neither," Piper responded.

"I expect you'll be getting used to it, once the world sees what a phenomenal artist you are."

"Holy shit! Look at all the people!" Piper said suddenly.

"And the cameras! Did you know that all the TV stations were covering this?" Devon was too startled to sound blasé.

"There's a red carpet! We are going to walk a freaking red carpet. I'm going to be sick." Piper swallowed hard.

"Don't you dare! Swallow it back if you have to! It's your big moment!"

The limo driver opened the door, Devon slid out and turned to give Piper his hand.

No sooner had she stood up, than a reporter was announcing that Piper McAllister, the new glass artist sensation, had arrived.

She and Devon slowly made their way up the red carpet, having to stop every few feet for pictures. Suddenly they were snagged for a quick interview by Lisa Blankly, the entertainment reporter from KTVU.. An assistant asked Devon his name and then passed them both over to Lisa.

"Piper, how excited are you for this first big showing?"

"Very excited, of course. What I am most excited about, of course is that The Gallery will finally be open. It is so beautiful inside and there are so many superior artists' work presented."

"I understand the large piece in the atrium is yours," pursued Lisa. "Can you tell us something about it?"

"Well, my initial inspiration came from my friend, Devon here. He's a writer. We'd been talking about writing, words and how a few words can make a difference. The piece is called 'From a Gathering of Glass.' I decided to incorporate words, art, glass and the fact that we are all originally much like molten glass, because our lives, the people we meet, the very air we breathe all become a part of us and the people we have the capacity to be."

"Well said," said Lisa, ending the interview. "Piper McAllister, the glass artist who is about to take the art world by storm."

"You handled that very well," said Devon under his breath as they continued up the red carpet.

"I'm surprised I even could get one word out."

Several more times they were stopped. Finally, they were escorted into The Gallery ahead of the invited guests, and Josh and Emily came forward to welcome them both.

"Don't you look lovely, Piper!" Emily enthused.

"Thank you. You do too! This is Devon Thorn, my friend and neighbor."

"The writer, right?" asked Josh.

Devon nodded, pleasantly surprised.

"After the rest of the artists arrive, then the crush will begin. Just mingle and smile and answer the same questions a hundred times or so. The art critics won't be here until later."

"Oh. I hadn't thought about the critics," Piper said to Devon a few minutes later. My father is one, but he's been on the east coast recently. Quite frankly, I'm not ready for this."

"You'll be fine and I expect your dad will be very proud of your work. He'd be crazy not to."

"But you don't understand," Piper began, only to be interrupted by Cee who had just said hello to Emily and Josh.

"Wow! You look amazing!" Cee said.

"You look ravishing, darling" Devon said twirling Cee about.

"Ravishing. I don't think anyone, ever, has called *me* ravishing!"

"More's the pity for a world full of imbeciles!" said Devon loyally. "You are glowing. Who is this with you?"

Cee grinned. "This is the love of my life and the most patient man on the planet! Devon, this is my husband, Galen. Galen, this is Devon and Piper. She does the glass sculptures."

The men greeted each other and Galen attempted to say something to Piper, but she'd already been pulled off to talk to someone else.

"Now Cee, you must show me your work. Galen, your wife is a brilliant artist!" Devon made the announcement as if there were a chance that Galen didn't already know it.

"Ohh," she blushed. "I will take you around, but would you mind," she said pulling the little group off towards the atrium, "if we go see this first? I saw it from outside, but I really want to see it from in he---Ohhh…"

Her voice dropped off and the three of them stood there, heads tilted up, looking at the sculpture lit up against the night sky. The only light in the atrium, it glittered and shone above them.

"Now THAT is a statement piece," whispered Cee to Devon. "Is that shorthand? It is. Let me see if I remember…"

"There is a transcription on the wall, see? Part way up the stairs. It's a poem."

"How perfect," Galen said, as they both read it.

"She really nailed it, didn't she?"

"Surely did. She surely did."

"Sweetheart," said Galen, "I want to go see the photography. I'll catch up with you in a bit." Giving her a quick kiss, he moved off through the rapidly building throng of people.

"Now," Devon continued, taking her arm, please do show me your work. Oh, my goodness! You have your own room! Haven't you just arrived! Oh, I love these. Oh! And this one!"

Devon moved around the room pausing and exclaiming before each piece. "I must have this one," he said pointing to one of two cats curled nose to tail like a feline yin and yang. "is it me, or are there several different themes going here? I am a Robin Williams fan and it seems to me that there's some imagery gleaned from his movies inspiring your work."

"There is," she smiled. "And I am a huge fan, ever since my mom made me watch 'Dead Poet's Society' when I was a kid."

"Oh I love that movie. So very sad about him. Such a loss. Oh. OH!" Devon's eyes lit on a drawing of a clock face that stunned him. He moved towards it as if he were being reeled in.

"CeeCee!"

Cee turned away from Devon's departing figure and turned toward the new voice.

"Mom, you're here!"

"Of course I am, where else would I be tonight?"

"Mom, this is Devon," Cee began. "Hmm... Well," she pointed, "He got sidetracked, I guess. Can't complain about that! Anyway, that's Devon over there. He is a friend of mine and he's Piper's escort tonight."

"Cee, just so you know that I know, your dad flew in for tonight as well. I don't think he's here yet, but he will be."

"Really? Wow. I never expected he'd fly in from Michigan. That is very cool!"

"Cee, is Galen with you?"

"He's off meandering. Ah, here's Devon again. Devon, this is my mother."

"Nice to meet you. Your daughter's work is amazing! Cee, since your mom's here, I'm going to go find Piper. I'll see you around, I'm sure."

With a quick wave, Devon headed off to locate Piper. He wandered around the various rooms, saw the rest of Piper's work, said hello to several of his friends, and finally found where the food was hiding. After filling the minuscule plate, he looked for a place to sit down. The only open chair was next to a man who sat there reading on his iPad. The man's brown shaggy hair was down in his eyes, and every time he swiped a page, he was pushing his hair out of his eyes. Devon walked over and sat.

"Hi. Always come to art gallery openings to read?"

"What? Oh. No. Too many people, kind of escaping for a few minutes."

"Good book?"

"Yes, actually. Epic fantasy. Ridiculously well thought out world in this one. It's by a relatively new author. Doesn't read newbie though. Excellent descriptions and layering."

"Really? I'm big on fantasy too. What's it called?"

"Downstream." It's about a world where there are rivers with currents too strong to go back up them, so all travel goes only…"

"One way and you can only go 'Downstream," Devon finished for him.

"You've read it then?

"No. I, ah, wrote it."

"You're Devon Thorn? Oh my god! I'm Garret, Garret Lord," he said, and they shook hands.

Twin thoughts bloomed in two minds. They smiled and began discussing the book, discussing other books – and the crowd of people vanished.

Piper charmed, listened, reacted, smiled and answered questions. She'd had several sips from several different glasses of champagne. As soon as she put one down on a tray, another was thrust into her hand by someone else. Several times she'd seen Devon and attempted to join him only to be intercepted by another guest. Once she'd seen him in deep conversation with some guy with hair in his eyes. So long, Byron, she thought, smiling. She'd given up even trying to remember names. She just nodded and acted as if she actually had a clue who some of these people were. Josh came up to her, extricated her from the current huddle of bodies and drew her off to meet the governor, who had just purchased her 'Puzzle' sculpture.

Peopled out momentarily, Piper sneaked off to the side of the room, where she finally found not only Devon, but food and the cute guy to whom Devon had been talking. Nibbling on an hors d'oeuvre, she listened to Devon introduce Garret and kept listening as he rattled off a list of celebrities who had come and told her half a dozen other things that she didn't hear. As soon as he stopped to take a breath, she jumped in.

"I met the governor," Piper gushed. "I met Lavern Cox and several others whom I'm sure I 'should' have recognized, but didn't. I just acted as if I knew who they were. Since they were, I'm almost positive, stars, they never noticed, assuming I knew who they were because, well, everyone (but me) does."

"Tonight, you are the star," said Joshua as he joined them. Every trip around, I've seen more and more of those discrete little sold signs we designed tucked by your work. You are going to be kept busy for quite a while replacing everything that's sold tonight!"

"Good thing I kept a few pieces back then! It'll be a month before my head is back down out of the stars!" Piper grinned – more relaxed than she had dreamed she could be at any Opening, much less this one.

"I met two of the three critics that should be here tonight. They both are very complimentary of your work. I'm looking forward to meeting the third, as I've been a fan of his for years. He's the one who inspired me to start painting."

Piper smiled. "It will be fun for you to meet him, then. You should tell him about inspiring you."

"I will, indeed," answered Josh. "Well, I'd best go mingle. Enjoy the opening."

Chapter 18

Phee stood on her balcony watching as Devon and Piper got into their limo. "Some people have all the luck," she muttered going for another drink. She finished the vodka and was halfway through the bottle of Jameson's. Returning to her chair outside, she sat down brooding. Nothing was going right. Nothing in her entire life was right. Never seeing Chloe. Eviction. Can't afford surgery. Can't. Not. Nope. Nothing. What did she have? Not a damn thing worth having. She sipped. Oh wait. She had three dollars and fifty-two cents in her purse. Didn't have another job scheduled for two weeks. What the hell was she going to do?

Someone, she didn't remember who, had told her she should go back to being a guy and then she could get a decent job. They didn't get it. They couldn't turn on and off that they were male or female. Why should she have to? It wasn't something one turned on and off like a switch. She was what she was, and what she was, inside, where it counted, was female. Life shouldn't be so hard. Maybe she should start that journal the shrink wanted her to do. Couldn't hurt, she supposed. Doubted it would help either. She sighed and downed the rest of the whiskey. It still burned on the way down. *Guess I'm not drunk enough yet.*

Four hours, a short nap and three more glasses of Jameson's later, Phee looked at what she'd written.

Journal of the Phoenix. I don't feel much like a phoenix any more. I sure as hell haven't risen from any ashes. I thought when I started my new life as a female that everything would be fine. I finally had the freedom to live as the female I am. I could dress as I pleased. Walk down the sidewalk in heels. Wear my hair long. Taking the hormones really helped. I didn't look so ... so male. I grew boobs. Nice boobs. So now I have boobs and a dick. What a mess! I look female. If you didn't know, you wouldn't know. I don't think that Piper chick has a clue. Must be nice to be so freely beautiful and never even have to think about it. Damn her to hell and back. It isn't fair.

Tried talking to Devon today. He's figured out, I think. He didn't really care either. Course, he's only gay —no big deal there. It's the in thing to be gay. It is still out to out oneself as trans. No way in hell the CIS upstairs would get it either. She's a bitch and isn't even trying to be one. I want to be her. All I'm good for is borrowed earrings. They could have invited me to go with them, but no. I'm not good enough I guess.

Today is Chloe's birthday. Her mother returned the birthday present I sent her ... didn't even open it; just wrote 'return to sender' on the box. Sender. She's my daughter. She's mine too. She's my little girl. God, I miss her.

Phee stopped reading and poured herself another drink. She stumbled on the way back to her bedroom. She looked at the big clock on the wall. *Blurry. Midnight. Wonder if Cinderella had fun at the ball? Of course she did. Star of the whole bloody show. Nope. Writing in the journal hadn't helped one god-damned bit. I feel worse now than I did earlier.*

"Think I'll take a bath while I still have one. She brought her journal, her drink and a candle into the bathroom. She started and adjusted the stream of water in the big claw-foot tub. Phee reached to the shelf, grabbed a jar of freesia-scented bubble bath, and dumped the whole bottle in the tub. *Bubbles hide what shouldn't be,* she thought.

Finishing the whiskey in her glass, she went to the kitchen and filled the glass full this time. A swallow or two hit the counter as her aim was off. She saw the bottle of valium on the window ledge. *Hell, why not. Damn liquor isn't helping. The valium relaxes me at least.* She had lots left. *Hell,* she thought, and popped five of them. Refilled her glass. *Least I will sleep tonight. It'd be nice to sleep. To sleep, perchance to dream. To be or not to be.* She giggled drunkenly.

Back in the bathroom, she lit the candle. She stripped off her clothes, let them drop. She looked down at them. More shells, more masks. *Why couldn't she just be?*

Phee climbed into the tub and sighed.

Chapter 19

Peter McAllister had taken several pages of notes. A tall man with bleached-out strawberry blond hair, he had worked his way from the Maidu section (he'd seen that artist's work before) and was now scribbling madly about the works of C.M. Baker.

He'd noticed Joey Domesco and Phyllis Abernathy, fellow critics, making the rounds. While he often disagreed with their opinions, he held them both in very high regard. Both loved the limelight, while he himself tended to try and slip beneath the radar, at least until he'd finished getting his opinions organized. He was happiest when he never even came in contact with the artists. He didn't want to see the hope in their eyes, listen to their questions or, occasionally, feel waves of dislike or fear roll off them.

C.M. Baker was a hit. No question there. Most every one of her pieces had a tiny 'sold' sign on it and she'd put together a rather unusual and cohesive showing of her work. He wouldn't mind having a piece or two of hers in his own private collection. He particularly liked her clear understanding how light both killed and created shadows, and her use of that knowledge. One of her pieces, a large clock-face drawn from an unusual angle, showed only the hours of ten through twelve, in Roman Numerals. Again, created through charcoal, it wasn't just the clock faces, but the shadows beneath the hands that made it so intriguing. She was young, but her potential was boundless.

Peter remembered Josh VanAllen's work from perhaps seven or eight years ago. He'd thought then that the young man had promise and Josh's more recent work showed he'd been right. His finesse with a brush had grown exponentially. He had an uncanny knack with depth and a way of pulling the viewer deep into the work. An eye for detail. Many artists tended to pay more attention to the center of the painting or, perhaps, to the area that was the focal point. With Joshua, the details were even, down to each leaf or beam of light. He was careful, precise, and very, very good.

Peter wished his son was here for this opening. He'd have enjoyed it –especially the glass exhibit, as he was interested in glass-work as well.

He'd seen the sculpture, 'From a Gathering of Glass' in the atrium, of course. You couldn't miss it. It was stunning, well executed and the artist was not afraid to stretch boundaries and add the unexpected touches. The use of shorthand to express the words was nothing short of brilliant. Five years from now, he imagined her pieces would be scattered across statement homes and businesses throughout Califor-nia, if not the world. There was no question about her becoming a major success. She was one artist he dearly wanted to meet.

His final stop would be the glass room. He'd saved it until last because every time he'd approached it, it had been too crowded with people, and he needed space to view the work. He glanced at his watch, pushing midnight. Surely, the crowd would have thinned a little with the late hour.

He saw the artist was in the room, but her back was turned and she was busy discussing something with, was that David Geffen? It most certainly was! Peter walked around her 'Day' and her 'Night,' appreciating the use of color. Both, he saw, had been sold. Her 'Swimming Against the Current' jelly fish certainly evoked move-ment. She was really a fine, fine artist. Her pieces invited that gentle touch, almost to reassure oneself of the reality of it. He finished his notes, all he ever used in his reviews and clicked send.

Seeing Davis Geffen walk out of the room, Peter turned to go up to the artist.

Back at Phee's apartment, she had written a little more in her journal, but the combination of too much alcohol and the valium were taking their toll.

I don't know what to do. Kinda hard to think right now. Everything's fuzzy. The bubbles are gone. No bubbles. I can see me and I don't like what I see.

The pen dropped out of Phee's fingers and landed in the water. She watched it float and then start to sink. She let her head lean back and rest on the towel at the edge of the tub. She was already sunk. Nothing was working any more. She didn't fit in anywhere or with anyone. She was stuck in some middle dimension that was neither here nor there, she was neither all male or all female and worse: she was a parent without a child.

Chapter 20

Peter turned to go meet the glass artist, a smile already on his face as his eyes met hers.

Unexpected recognition shocked his soul. A crushing pain bloomed in his chest. Piper was startled as her eyes met those of the man walking towards her. *Father? He was supposed to be on the east coast.* She knew this moment was coming; but here? Now? She wasn't ready for this.

There was no air in the room. He couldn't breathe. His last thought before blacking out was, *Why is my son wearing a dress?*

Piper staggered backward, as if someone or something had shoved her back. That look of absolute disdain she saw in his eyes was devastating.

A woman screamed, startling her back into the moment. "Father!"

Piper ran forward, crouched at his side. She heard someone calling 911. Another man yelled, "I'm a doctor," as he pushed through the crowd, telling people to move back. He took Peter's pulse, bent over and listened for air. On his knees, the man pulled open Peter's jacket and began CPR.

Devon, following the noise, came to Piper's side. "My father."

"What?"

"He's my fa-father. I didn't, I never expected to see him here. He doesn't know—" her voice dropped off.

"Doesn't know what?"

"Oh Devon. He thinks...he's...This is all my fault." Piper was now openly crying. Mascara ran down her cheeks in a single stream.

"Move, everyone. Move back now. The EMTs are here. Miss, you need to move back."

"He's my father. I need to go with him. Will he be all right?"

"I don't know, Miss. You need to move back." Seeing Devon with his arm around the shaking Piper, he continued, "Sir, please take her out front. She can go with the ambulance. Right now, we need to do our jobs."

Devon guided Piper through the crowd and out the front door. "You go with him. I'm sure everything'll be fine. You okay? You are awfully pale."

"He," she paused. "He doesn't know. Remember when you made that 'years of shopping comment and I said I had something to tell you? He doesn't know."

"Darling, I have no idea what you are talking about." He hugged her as that seemed the best thing to do at the moment.

"He doesn't know. Dev, the last time he saw me," she cried into his shoulder. "The last time he saw me I was his son."

Devon straightened. Lights blinked on, comments fell into place, and his heart ached for her. "Oh. Well. Ah." *What on earth was he to say? Could say, should say?* "Well, love, the cat's out of the bag, now. Um. Are you sure you want to ride with him? Maybe it would be better if you met him at the hospital, see how he's doing. Take the limo. Want me to come with you?"

"No, I need to handle this. I can ... handle this. You're right, I'd better take the limo. If he's conscious in the ambulance, it will freak him out. God. Dev. I might have killed my father!"

"Not intentionally. You didn't expect to see him here. You need to calm down."

He called for the limo so it could follow the ambulance. When it pulled up, he got her inside and handed her a bottle of water. "Drink this," he said, handing it to her. He then explained to the limo driver more or less what was going on.

"Do you want me to wait for the lady, sir?"

"No, just drop her off. I'll get her when she's ready to come home." The driver nodded and got back in the vehicle.

Inside, EMTs worked on Peter McAllister. Emily and Josh stood at the edge of the crowd, watching.

Emily looked from the man on the gurney to her husband. Seeing them almost side by side reminded her of a thought earlier in the evening when she'd first met the art critic. Now wasn't the time, but there was no escaping the fact to her. Joshua obviously wasn't seeing it, but there was no doubt in Emily's mind at all.

The men ran for the entrance with the gurney and began loading him into the ambulance.

"How is he, sir? I need to tell his dau…er. Hmmm."

"He's stabilized. Where's the girl?"

"She'll follow you to the hospital in the limo."

"Okay then, let's roll," he said climbing in. The other EMT shut the door, got in the front. Sirens blaring, they drove off down the road, the limo right behind.

Chapter 21

Devon hailed a cab. When he got to the house, he was reminded of their earlier promise to stop and tell Phee about the evening. It was late, but all her lights were on, so he felt he at least needed to stop in and fill her in on part of the evening.

Arriving on the second floor, he knocked on Phee's door. When she didn't answer, he knocked again and then tried the knob. It turned, unlocked as promised. He went in.

"Phee? Phee, I'm back. Hello?"

Every light blazed, but there was no answer. He checked the couch, in case she'd fallen asleep there but it was empty. He checked her bedroom and then knocked on the closed bathroom door. "Phee?"

Still no answer. Cracking the door open, he peered inside before rushing in.

"Phee! Oh dear god." She was in the tub, slid down with half her face in the water. He shook her, but her head just lolled back and forth. He felt for a pulse and felt one, barely. "Phee! Wake up!" No response. Devon pulled out his phone and called 911. He gave them the information and, on hearing they'd be right there, he ran back downstairs to open the house's front door.

He hurried back upstairs and went back into the bathroom.

He looked at Phoenix in the tub and reached to support her head so that it wouldn't go under water. Seeing her naked body under the water was when he realized fully the significance of what she'd told him earlier in the day. *Quite the night,* he thought, before telling himself that it was not funny. *Not at all.*

Hearing the EMTs coming in the apartment, he met them and got out of the way. *Her purse, she'd need her id.*

"Is she okay?"

"We don't know yet. You coming with?"

"Yes. Ah. I'll follow you. I'll meet you there. Here's her ID."

"You her … um … her …"

"No. I live upstairs."

"Let's get moving then." Devon noticed they'd put her journal on the gurney.

They brought her down to the ambulance as Devon went to get his car. *It's by the grace of God I didn't go with Piper to the hospital,* he thought.

Neither of the EMTs working on Phee noticed the barely discernable Jinn in the ambulance with them.

Chapter 22

Arriving at the hospital shortly after the ambulance, Devon tried to follow Phee to where they were taking her. "You family?"

"No, I'm her —"

"Sorry, only family."

Devon stared at the swinging doors for a long moment, and then went to see if he could find Piper.

He found her, sitting all by herself, curled into a comfortable looking and oversized chair in a waiting room down from the ER.

"Hey."

"What are you doing here?"

"Talking to you. How's your dad?"

"They say he's stable, for the moment. They are taking him for an EKG or something."

"I should have brought you something to change into. I wasn't thinking."

"Why'd you come?"

"Ah, Piper, Phee's here too."

"What?"

"I stopped by to see her as we said we would. I found her, out cold in her tub. I couldn't wake her up, so I called 911. I didn't know what else to do. Pipe, when I found her, she was this close (he motioned with his hands) to sliding completely under the water."

"Oh my god. She okay?"

"I don't know. I'm not family, they wouldn't let me follow her. I shoulda lied."

"Yeah."

"Piper, you know I don't care you are—"

"Transgender."

"Yeah," he nodded. You know I know, right? You are just Piper."

"My father won't think so. I was his only son. He's a bit chauvinistic, you could say. He always was telling me how proud he was of having a son. Never wanted a daughter. Then, after mom died having me, he always said her last gift to him was me, a son. I guess I took that away from him."

"You need to be who you are, Piper. Remember that, okay?"

"I'll try. So, what about Phee?"

"Yeah. Piper, she's ah, transgender too. She hasn't had surgery yet, though." Devon looked at her questioningly, then blushing, he turned his head.

"It's okay, Dev. I have. I'm all female now." She smiled. "I remember how I looked before…half in one world, half in another."

"Kind of took me aback for a moment, but then, all I've ever known her as is Phee. So she's Phee."

"I hope she's okay. Oh, here comes the doctor."

"Want me to leave?"

"No. Please stay."

"Ms. McAllister?" She nodded. "Your father had a cardiac infarction. Two of his arteries are almost totally blocked. He will be going in for surgery almost immediately. While there are no guarantees, he should be okay, we think. He is unconscious still, but do you want to see him for a moment before we take him upstairs?"

"Yes, please." She followed them into a room full of machines that blinked and beeped. He looked smaller than he usually did in her eyes. Of course, she hadn't seen him asleep in years. He never seemed to sleep much. He was always busy, always on the run, always in a hurry. She felt the nurse take her arm. "Love you, Dad," she said as she was gently pulled away.

On the other side of the hospital, in the psychiatric emergency room, Phee lay strapped to the gurney with an IV bag running liquids into her arm. Her chest was wired to a heart monitor.

"The EMTs gave me this, Doctor." The nurse handed him the journal the EMTs had brought with them.

Jinn, perched atop the heart monitor machine, listened to the doctor while her eyes stayed glued to Phee.

"They were thinking possible suicide or perhaps accidental suicide attempt. I'll be sure Doctor Schedley gets this. He's her counselor for her sexual reassignment surgery."

The nurse nodded.

"She's in a coma. She came very close to dying today. All we can do at the moment is keep our eyes and monitors on her and hope for the best," he said as they both left the room.

Left alone, the unconscious Phee was somehow aware that "alone" was not quite the right word.

"Am I in heaven?"

"No," came the reply.

"Am I dead?"

"No."

"Then why are *you* here?"

"To help you." Phee could barely see the figure who replied to her, but she *could* sense her.

"Who are you? Are you an angel?"

"My name is Jinn. No, I am not an angel. You aren't dead, yet. "

"Where am I?" Phee wanted to know.

"You're in the hospital," Jinn replied.

"Are you a ghost? Are you dead?"

"Yes."

That was too much. "If *I'm* not dead, how can I talk to you? "

"Because you're in a coma," Jinn answered. "What happens next will be up to you. Nothing is certain yet. Know, at the moment, you are safe. Rest now."

Phee slept. The monitors beeped on.

Chapter 23

A gentle hand touched Piper's shoulder.

"Ms. McAllister, your father came through surgery. He's conscious and asking for his son, for Peter. Is your brother coming?"

"Ah…" She looked over to Devon helplessly. "That's kind of complicated. I am, er, was Peter," she began. "No easy way 'round this. I'm transgender, post-operative. My father didn't know until he saw me last night, which he may not even remember having done. But when he saw me, that's when he had his heart attack."

"Hmm. I think perhaps I should clear this with his doctor first. You hang tight. I'm going to go talk with Doctor Daniels. I'll be back."

The nurse scurried off, a worried look on her face.

"I can see it now," Piper said softly, "Trans woman accused of murder after shocking unsuspecting father with transformation."

Devon shook his head. "I get that it was a surprise, a shock even, but if he loves you, everything should be all right."

"No, it won't. I mean, yeah, he loves me, or should I say, he loves Peter. He doesn't know Piper, who is who I am and who I have been. He loves the 'concept' of the *son*. It's that 'a man and his son' rhetoric. To make matters worse, in *his* mind, through *his* eyes, even as a son I barely measured up. 'Course, that's probably because in *my* eyes, I wasn't his son, but his daughter. It's a mess."

It was at least an hour later when Dr. Daniels joined Piper and Devon in the waiting room.

"Hi. I'm Dr. Daniels, your father's doctor. I understand we have something of a complicated mess to unravel here. Piper, am I to understand that your father had no knowledge of your being transgender?"

"No, he didn't. I've been out of the country until recently and we've had very little contact. He is always so busy on the road, that there just never seemed to be the right time. It isn't the sort of thing you want to tell your dad over the phone, and we haven't actually seen each other in three years. Mostly, we've communicated by email. Dad's not much of a phone person to begin with and we've never really had the family things going on. I figured out pretty early on that this was a subject that was not going to go over well. He simply was not going to understand. It would be a phase I was going through or I'd be acting out or I was trying to ruin his life. I had no idea he'd be there last night. As far as I knew, he was on the east coast. If I'd known, I would have worked out a way to let him know, get together with him or something. Now, I feel so guilty."

"Well, on one level, you probably saved his life. This heart attack was coming whether it was due to a shock or tripping as he crossed a room or when he heard a sound that startled him. Luckily he had it where the emergency response was immediate. If he'd been alone, he'd be dead. He needs to know that and I will tell him so.

"I think he needs a bit more healing time before you two talk, assuming you want to do that."

She nodded. "We do need to talk. I just don't want to hurt him again."

"You didn't hurt him. Shock him, yes. But you really did make a silent killer obvious and in doing so, you helped your dad in the long run. I think, maybe, in a day or so, I will bring this up, see what he remembers from last night and see how it goes. He may not even want to see you. I'm sorry if that hurts, but if that is the case, I will abide by his wishes."

"I understand that," she said sadly. "It was always about the 'son' thing with him. According to my dad, it was the sons that mattered to a man, only the sons would carry on the name, the family. He once told me he was glad I'd been a son because sons were important to a man. So his son really being a woman inside and now, outside as well, will be very difficult for him to handle, to understand – let alone to accept."

The doctor nodded slowly. "You may as well go home. Obviously, under the circumstances, you can't see him, but I will keep you informed, make sure the nurses are apprised that they can give you updates, etc. I will talk to you soon. Don't worry though, your dad will be okay."

Saying that, Dr. Daniel walked back towards the nurses station. Piper slumped in her seat.

"Maybe we could go see how Phee is doing?"

"Will they even tell us?"

"I don't know. Maybe her mom will have come. We could talk to her."

"That's a good idea."

Devon and Piper walked over to the other side of the hospital. Checking in at the nurse's station at the outer entrance to the psychiatric ward, they were told that Phee's mother was indeed there and was in a waiting room down the hall.

They went into the waiting room. It was decorated in what one might assume to be calming greens. There were plastic chairs that looked as if they were middle school rejects. The greens had aged into what only could be the color of bile. Two women sat uncomfortably near a coffee table strewn with decade's-old teen magazines, or that's what they were if the bell-bottomed, crocheted vested model on the cover gave any clue.

"Hi. We are sorry to disturb you, but are you Phee's mother?"

asked Piper.

The tired-looking woman looked up. Her eyes were red and swollen. "Yes."

"We are Piper and Devon. Our apartments are upstairs from Phee. Devon," Piper motioned, "found Phee. How is she?"

"She's in a coma," said the worried woman. "They don't know when or if she will come out of it."

Piper sat. "I am so sorry. She was up in my apartment this afternoon. We saw her as we were leaving for the opening, and she told us to come by when we got home if her lights were on."

"I saw lights, knocked, and then went in when she didn't answer," added Devon.

"Thank God you did! I'm Laine, Bob-eh-Phee's sister." Laine reddened, embarrassed by the slip.

Devon smiled. "We know," he said kindly. "She's been a bit stressed of late, but we didn't know she was this upset. Thinking back to when I found her, it certainly didn't look like a suicide, more like she passed out in the tub."

"The doctors said they found what they feel is a suicide note in her journal."

"I know her counselor was having her keep a journal. She told me about that when she was upstairs yesterday afternoon. She came up for coffee," Devon offered. "She seemed down, but not *down*, if you know what I mean."

"It is a fairly normal thing to be counseled to keep a journal. The over-riding hope is that transgendered people will write down thoughts and work through them. They might write down what they are feeling at any given moment, but even when they write it, it doesn't necessarily mean they are going to kill themselves after a horrible week. Those are just temporary feelings that most people have and don't act on. Obviously, some people do, but the journals are to be seen by the counselors. If someone were actively in crisis, it is probably the last thing they'd write, but if they were planning on committing suicide, it typically would be spelled out, or a rant or a 'last words' sort of thing."

"It just doesn't make any sense to me," her mother said. "Why would she do this when she was worried about spending time with Chloe? This isn't going to help at all," she finished sadly.

"Let's hope when she wakes up she tells us she got drunk and passed out. That is far better than the alternative. She wouldn't be the first or last person to do that," said Laine.

"Her doctor was mentioning all sorts of facts and figures about suicide in pre-surgical transgenders and that the number of suicides is very high," Phee's mom said.

"They are," Piper said. "Actually, pre-surgery numbers are between three to five times the national averages. Stress over affording surgery, issues with exes over marital children, and difficulties with finding and keeping jobs in a world that isn't quite ready for the transgender woman in a workplace add inordinate stresses. It is getting better though. Slowly, but acceptance levels are growing."

"Seems like you hear every week about a star or celebrity who is transgender," Laine commented. "You hear about kids now who are. Seems as if there is less compulsion to hide it."

"Yes," Piper agreed. "Hiding it used to be what one had to do at all costs. At least it is nowhere near as bad as it was twenty or ten or even five years ago. Phee was most of the way through her initial hormone replacement therapy, at least as close as I can figure," she went on. "The counseling was the last step before she could be recommended for her reassignment surgery. She did have a lot on her plate. Any transwoman does. The world doesn't get it, yet. People don't understand that it isn't a choice, it simply is."

Laine looked over to Piper, considering. "You sound as if you really know what you are talking about."

Piper looked her straight in the eyes, answering, "I do."

"Oh," replied Laine.

Chapter 24

"You're still here?"

"Yes," answered Jinn. "I'm not going anywhere."

"Still in a coma, huh?"

Jinn nodded.

"You said you were dead, but you didn't answer me before. Are you in Heaven, well, when you aren't sitting on the foot of my bed?"

Jinn sighed. "Sort of."

"What's it like? Heaven, I mean."

"I'm not, ah hmmm. I'm not all the way in yet. Sometimes, there are things you are asked to do."

"Never really got it, Heaven I mean. You've got all these different religions and all of them have their ideas about Heaven or Valhalla or the afterlife. Doesn't make any sense to me."

"That part's easy," smiled Jinn. "Pretty much everyone has heard how God has a 'mansion with many rooms.' Well, imagine a really huge house with tons of rooms in it. Each religion has its own suite, so to speak."

"Ohh. That makes sense, but isn't it awfully crowded? Billions upon billions of people have died in the last two thousand years."

"When you get inside, you change. Because I'm here, with

you, I haven't been 'inside' yet. I'm kinda in the courtyard still. But inside, you don't really need your body anymore, or don't care about it so much. Walking through those front doors, your priorities change, I guess. Anyway, your soul or the spark that is you is what is there. Imagine your mind as a... a... firefly maybe. Something like that. And each room is far beyond what you can imagine."

"How do you find anyone? Like grandparents or friends?"

"Well, each spark has the good memories and emotions. You think about the loved one and you find them. I don't know too much about how it all works yet, but when you are first there, the sparks whizz around finding Mom or Dad or a grandparent. But after a while, you just don't think about it as much. You remember, it's like you kind of peek out the windows to check on the living now and then, but your soul becomes full of other things."

"Oh. It's kind of nice to know that."

"You can't really go around telling people either. They won't believe you or they'll think you're crazy. You don't need any more of that."

"I'm not crazy!"

"You're in the psychiatric ward of the hospital because you tried to commit suicide, Phee."

"I did? I don't remember. How'd I do it?"

"Drank too much, took too many valiums, took a bath and passed out."

"I remember now. I was just trying to relax, to make all my problems go away, not kill myself. I wouldn't do that."

"Consciously or subconsciously? You're not stupid, Phee. Pretty much a given that you don't mix valium with liquor. Everybody knows that!"

"Like you never did anything stupid when you were alive? Give me a break. It's probably why you're here with me."

Jinn smiled. "Pretty much. Phee, what I did or didn't do isn't the point. What *you* did is. Trying to cover it up or making excuses will not help you. Do you remember what you wrote in your journal?"

Phee didn't say anything for a moment. "I didn't mean to write..."

"But you did."

"Yeah, guess I did. I can't even see my daughter. I can't get a decent job and, without the job, I'm getting evicted and I'll never be able to afford surgery. I need to be all me, not some circus freak sideshow halfway between now and never! So yeah, guess maybe I did."

"So it is all about you?"

"Yes, it is."

No, it isn't. You don't live in a vacuum, Phee. There is more to Phee, and who you are than a little bunch of temporary setbacks."

"Little to you, maybe," Phoenix made a face. "Not to me."

"Not in the grand scheme of things. There's a saying: You are more than the sum of your parts. You need to consider that. Rest now and think. I'll see you in a bit."

Phee grew sleepy. "But I don't want to..." she began. And she slept.

Chapter 25

"Good morning, love," Galen said, as he blearily opened his eyes and realized it was almost noon. "How's my star today?"

"Dead. I died. I had to have died or I'd feel better than I do. Headache," Cee moaned.

"We aren't used to these late nights that don't end until the wee hours of the morning. I don't think we got to bed until something after three."

"Ugh." Cee rolled over and attempted to bury her head under her pillow. "No wonder I feel so dead. Move, Caboodle," she ordered the black and white cat who was fighting her for the pillow.

The cat just purred, dug in her claws and placidly refused to let go. Cee moaned.

Sounding far too cheerful and awake for her tastes, her husband offered to go get her some aspirin.

"Oh, please. I'll love you forever."

"You would anyway unless my rising star plans to leave me in her charcoal dust for someone rich and famous."

"No chance, babe. There isn't another man on the planet as loving, cat crazy and patient as you are. The rich and famous are good for buying my artwork…."

"… Which they did in droves last night. You are going to be

the invisible wife 'til you create a bunch more work to replace it. Still can't get over those two guys outbidding each other when you said that you wouldn't reproduce one of your pieces. What did you end up getting for the clock piece anyway?"

"Three times what I put on it. Then, I told the other gentleman, privately, that, if he liked, I would create a similar piece for him at the original price, on commission. Hell of a life," she giggled, taking the aspirin and slugging down some water.

"Not so much for Piper and, was that her father?"

"I don't know. She seemed awfully upset and he went down right after he saw her, at least according to what I heard."

"Last names are the same."

"Oh. I didn't realize that. Must be. But why should that be a problem? You'd think she'd happy he came."

"From what I heard, he was totally shocked to see her there at all."

"Whatever happened, I expect we will hear about it at some point."

Chapter 26

Monday morning. Emily pushed another one of The Gallery reviews out of the way and put down her coffee cup. Josh looked up from the cat in his lap and said, "Em, do you think we should go to the hospital and see how Peter McAllister is doing? Bring flowers or something?"

Emily remained sitting and busied herself stacking the recently cut out articles to buy herself some time. She'd been wanting to say something to Josh ever since she'd seen Peter lying on the floor with the EMTs bustling around him.

She wondered if her impressions of the man would have been different if she'd met him while he was walking around The Gallery. She didn't know and that just layered the strange feelings she was having. While she wasn't positive, she was ninety percent sure she was right, but that didn't make the idea of bringing it up to Josh any easier, especially since he, obviously, hadn't seen what she had at all.

"Sure, we could send flowers," she said absentmindedly.

"Send. Instead of going?"

"Well, he did just have a heart attack. He might not be up for visitors. I wonder why he had it just then, did something happen? Piper was awfully upset. Does she know him?"

"I don't think so. Though, there is that last name thing. Maybe she's a niece or a cousin or something."

"Kinda strange."

"Yeah."

Emily poured them both some more coffee. "Josh, where's that art book, the one McAllister wrote?"

"Upstairs, somewhere, why?

"Could you go get it?"

"Ah, sure. Why?"

"I'm curious about something."

Josh went upstairs and came back a few minutes later. "I haven't even looked at this book in years. Back, before we met, I don't think a week would go by when I wasn't opening it for some reason or another. Strange, huh?"

Taking the book when he handed it to her, she flipped it over to look at the back. Then opening it, she looked at the back flap of the dust jacket. No. Not a doubt in the world.

"Josh, did you look at Peter when he was having his heart attack?"

"Yes, why?"

"You looked at his face?"

"He was awfully gray. I was afraid he was dead."

"No, I mean, did you 'look' at him?"

"Em, what are you talking about? I just told you I did."

She handed Josh the book, opened, so he could see the author bio and picture on the back flap.

"Yeah, so?"

She sighed, shook her head. "Come with me."

Josh followed her to the half bath off the kitchen. She pointed to the mirror. "Look."

Josh looked at the book and then in the mirror. The face staring back was almost a mirror image of Peter McAllister twenty years younger, as he had been when he wrote the book.

Josh's eyes met those of Emily in the mirror. The color had drained from his face. Again, his eyes went back and forth from the picture to his reflection.

"Do you think?" His voice trailed off. "No, it can't be, can it?"

"You said you never knew who your real father was."

"I didn't know that my step-father wasn't my real dad until after both he and my mother were dead."

"Did you buy this book?"

"No, actually, my mother gave it to me as a birthday present. Em," he said sounding almost lost. "She had to have known."

"So. What do you want to do now?"

"I don't know. It's not every day that your heretofore unknown father drops in his tracks at your gallery. I've got so many questions."

"Well, at some point," Em told him logically, "if you want the answers, you will need to talk to him."

"Sure, just walk into the guy's hospital room and say, "Hey there. Not that your system has had any stress lately, but I think I'll add some more to it. I think you are my dad.""

"Yeah, that might not be the best way to handle it. Maybe you could ask him if he knew your mom," Em suggested.

"That'd bring an interesting reaction, I bet. Unless of course, this is just a weird coincidence and he doesn't know her."

"Josh, we're talking mirror images here," she said pointing at the picture.

He sighed. "Did he know Mom was pregnant? Did he just leave when he found out? Did Mom break up with him and just not tell him? Sometimes, Em, I feel as if my whole life was just piles of secrets layered on top of one another; each one hiding something else. After Jukai I thought we'd hit the bottom of the secret box."

"I guess not," she said, giving him a hug. "We've sure had our share of them."

"I wonder if Grandmother Alice knew."

"Somehow, I expect she did."

"Yeah, me too."

Chapter 27

Peter McAllister painfully moved his shoulder trying to shift position. He couldn't get comfortable. Everything hurt. He felt weak as a child, although he could breathe better and felt better than he had in ages ... as long as he remembered not to move. He hated hospitals. He didn't like feeling helpless, attached to wires and IVs. The monitors beeped annoyingly, changing their cadence every time he moved or shifted. Sometimes they beeped even when he didn't.

The last few days were little more than a blur. He remembered being at The Gallery opening and then waking up here after having had surgery. There were bits and pieces, fragments, seconds of ... something happening. He'd seen Peter, hadn't he? Something there. But the images his mind played back were like a slideshow in fast forward. Images of pieces from the show, people, Peter, some girl with red hair, sculptures, sounds, alarms, sirens and the babble of too many people talking at once. He couldn't separate them; they all ran together like a rainstorm hitting a tilted sidewalk covered in chalk drawings. He shook his head, but he couldn't focus. It was too tiring trying to think. He slept.

He awakened to his doctor's voice and with a picture in

his mind of Peter superimposed over the redhead he vaguely remembered. The redhead was Peter.

The monitors went crazy as the beeping increased to a fevered pitch. "Mr. McAllister, you need to calm down. Are you in pain?"

"Peter. My son." The monitors kicked it up another notch and Mr. McAllister began gasping for breath. The nurse ran into the room. Responding to the doctor's instructions, she inserted a syringe of medication into her patient's IV. Within seconds, his breathing slowed and he visibly relaxed.

Puzzled, he looked at the doctor. "I think I'm having delusions or something. I keep seeing images of my son dressed like a woman. But that's impossible. I need to see him, I want to see Peter."

"Mr. McAllister, there is no easy way to tell you this. You son is transgender. Do you know what that is?"

"What, he's a fag or something?"

Dr. Daniel hid the immediate cringe. "No, sir. Transgendered individuals have the outward appearance of one gender, but inside, in their minds, with all they are, all of their being, they are the opposite gender."

"So he thinks he's a girl? My Peter? Impossible. Must just be a phase or something. He must be on drugs. I'll get him a shrink to fix his head."

"It isn't like that, sir. It is not something that can be 'fixed' away. It isn't Peter's choice. In the womb, we are wired male or female. Sometimes the shell doesn't fit the hard-wiring of the brain. Likely, your son has felt "different" his entire life, but hid it from you, your family, even from himself for a while until the feelings became so strong he had to do something about them."

"Not Peter. He's my son, my only child."

"Your son had surgery several years ago. Peter is now physically, emotionally and," he paused, "legally a woman. Her name is Piper. I also need to tell you that she was not expect-ing to see you Saturday evening. She thought you were in New York. She is feeling terribly guilty that you suffered your heart attack when you saw her. "

"He, she, whatever the fuck it is should. I could have died. Whatever that mutation is would have killed me."

"Mr. McAllister. Stop. You need to know that, quite possibly, she saved your life. Your heart attack was a given, considering the state your heart was in. Had you had your attack driving, or while home alone, or while you were asleep, you would not be here. You would be dead. Only the fact that you were able to get immediate care saved your life."

"No. I do not want to hear that. An abomination, that's what it –"

"Sir," the doctor interrupted. "I realize this takes some getting used to. It is quite an adjustment you need to make, to accept."

"I don't know if I can. I don't know if I even want to."

"Well, if you loved your son, you might want to think about it. Granted, this has been an emotional shock, but it is a fact. From what I've heard, she's an exceptional artist. I've met her, you know. She's a lovely woman. Maybe you could think about giving her a chance. And keep in mind that this wasn't a spur of the moment decision on her part. It is something she's lived with her entire life. She's spent years going through the process that included psychological evaluations, hormone therapy and surgery. It took a lot of guts. It was not an easy decision for her to make the changes she needed to make herself feel complete.

The doctor looked at Peter closely. "Your medication is kicking in, you need to rest. I will check in with you later. Piper wants to see you. I told her it was up to you, your decision, your call. Sleep on it, think about it."

"I don't want to think about it. My son is now my daughter?" He shuddered. "Who'd want to think about that?"

"You will, sir. Whether it's the he that Peter was or the she that Piper is, we're talking about your child."

Chapter 28

Emily sat out on the deck thinking. Everything was haywire, canted just enough out of kilter to make her feel she was standing halfway outside herself. Josh had gone for a walk three hours ago. He was a mess, she could tell; he didn't know which side was up.

His mother had never told him who his real father was, letting him believe that the jerk she'd married was his real father. Yet she gave him the book. Why? In hopes he'd still have it as an adult and might figure things out? If it hadn't been for his seeing Piper, they still wouldn't know.

Mothers. You were supposed to be able to trust your mother—no matter what. Yet neither of them had been able to do that. Were their particular mothers doing what they did out of love? Or was it out of selfishness? They'd never truly know.

Emily pondered further. She had a twin she'd been cheated out of. Thanks to her mother giving up, giving away Jinn, the twins never had a chance to share more than a moment or two with each other. Her mother did not have the right to play with other people's lives. Josh's mother should have told him the truth and given him the chance, the choice, but she'd hoarded her secret every bit as much as Emily's mother had kept hers. And, as a result, both Emily and Josh had big empty holes where sisters and fathers should have been.

Josh was out walking, trying to deal, Em knew, with the fact that he had a sister and a father, neither of whom even knew about his existence. Em figured that Josh's mom must never even have let Peter McAllister know she was pregnant with his child – just as her own mother never let her know she had a sister. It was so intrinsically wrong. How, why would, could people do such things? It was beyond her.

The only one who knew, or apparently knew, about all of it from every side was her Grandmother Alice. Alice had tried as best she could to let the pieces of the puzzles at least have some hope of coming together.

Em absent-mindedly scratched Sherry's ears. *Do you know? You've been around forever now. Did Grandma talk to you? Do you have the answers?*

What if Josh and I had committed suicide? All those pieces would have fallen through the cracks. So much might had died right then. Emily shook her head. It was just too much. So many thoughts were tumbling and tangling. If only Jinn hadn't died. She really could use a sister right about now.

"Emily, I'm here."

Emily looked up, around. There, standing at the railing of the deck was Jinn. Her sister.

"Jinn."

"I want to hug you."

"I know. Me too." Jinn looked down at, through, herself. "Yeah. That's not going to happen."

"Everything is such a mess."

"I know it really seems that way, right now. But you have Joshua and the two of you will get through this together. Look," she pointed at the sliding glass doors behind them.

Emily could see them both reflected there, standing side by side. She smiled.

"I don't know how long I can be here. But for now, know I am nearby."

"Are you here now because of all this?"

"No, not really. I'm here for something else, someone else, but while I am, at least we can talk and see each other. Nothing will ever be able to make up for what we lost. We only have the now to make the best of what we can have going forward."

"Emma really can see you?"

"Yes, she can," Jinn smiled. "She looks very much like I did at her age. She is very much like I was. In a way, you will be able to see a bit of what you missed. Oh, and Em, I warn you: I was a real brat!"

They laughed together. Meeting Jinn's eyes, Emily felt as if her heart would overflow.

"I love you, Sis."

"Yeah, me too, you. I need to go, but I'll be back. Josh'll be okay, he just will really need you now, even when he thinks he doesn't. Be there, as we couldn't be for each other."

"I will. Bye," Emily said as Jinn melted away.

Chapter 29

Phee opened her eyes and saw Jinn over in the corner of the room. She looked sad, thought Phee.

"You look sad."

"I am, a little. Missing what never was, still can't be. Have you done any thinking?

"Yes, but it hasn't solved anything. In here at least, I don't have to deal with much except you dropping in out of nowhere."

"Consider this a rest stop. You still will have to finish your journey, one way or the other. Come on. You and I are going to take a trip."

"Hello? Coma. Can't move."

Jinn held out her hand to Phee. "Take my hand. Come."

"What is this, like some weird version of *A Christmas Carol?*"

Jinn grinned. "No, more like *It's a Wonderful Life.* But very different. No one but Clarence even knew what George Bailey got to see. Hard as knowing what life would be without him was for George, this will be harder for you. Come."

Phee and Jinn stood in a room with high ceilings. Tall windows were draped in deep mulberry, velvet curtains that barricaded the people within from hearing any sounds without.

They also trapped in the sounds of crying, sniffling and anger.

Phee saw her sisters crying. She saw her brothers standing uncomfortably over on the other side of the room. Their eyes kept darting around, looking anywhere but in the coffin.

"I will never forgive you for this," her mother hissed to her father. "You have never accepted her. She was never good enough for you, was she?"

"She's a he, no matter how screwed up he was. He was my son, not your daughter. It's probably all your fault he ended up like this. Why'd you encourage him in this nonsense?"

"Encourage? At first all I did was DIScourage him. But when I learned more about what was going on, I realized that she had to do what felt right for her. Not for you. Not for me. For herself!"

"And look where that got him. Dead. In a box."

"Maybe if you'd offered our child some support, some understanding. But no. You had to be the big chief male, who couldn't begin to fathom that for some people, that is the very last thing they are meant to be."

"Don't try to sell me that psychobabble. I'm not buying it. You think I'm stupid? You are the stupid one if you think any of this was anything more than a bunch of excuses to get out of being a man."

Phee stared. She was shaking. She wanted to yell, to scream. But when she tried, she realized she couldn't say a word.

"They can't hear you. They can't see you. You can't touch them."

"There are things I need to say. Maybe unpleasant things, but my father needs to know them. I don't care if he hates me; he needs to know my mother did the right things in trying to help me."

"You can't do that in a coma, can you?"

Jinn pulled Phee over to the coffin.

"No, I don't want to look. I don't want to see."

"Look. See. Understand," said Jinn firmly.

Phee looked down at the coffin. There was a man lying there with short dark hair, wearing a suit. "That's not who I am. That is not me."

Phee's mother came over to kneel at the side of the coffin. "I am so sorry, dear. I tried, but he over-ruled me. You don't even look like you, like my Phee."

"It isn't me. I am not that person. I am here, Mother. It isn't me! It isn't me!" Crying now, she didn't resist as Jinn pulled her over to where her sisters sat huddled together.

"I should have noticed something. I should have done something."

"I feel so guilty. How could we not have known things were so bad for her? Didn't she know she could have come to us?"

Phee felt her heart break a little, but she said to Jinn, "Couldn't they have offered?"

"Couldn't you have asked?" Jinn pulled her over to the display of flowers near the coffin. " Look, Phee. Remember."

Jinn took Phee's hand again. Phee and Jinn were in a bedroom. A college diploma hung on a wall. A woman came through the door with Phee's sisters. She was wearing a wedding gown that made her look every bit the princess she'd always been in Phee's mind.

"Chloe."

"It's her wedding day. She is marrying a wonderful man. You'd be very proud of both of them."

Chloe stopped the women fussing at her. "I need a moment." As the women left the room, Chloe went over to her dresser and took out a photo in a frame that had been buried at the bottom of a drawer.

"Daddy. Daddy, I have never cared that you were a woman! You are still my daddy. Why aren't you here? Man, woman, you still should be here. You should be walking me down the aisle today." Tears streamed down Chloe's face, mascara running in rivulets down her cheeks, splashing onto the white gown, leaving streaks. "You should be here. Why aren't you? How could you leave me? I was a little kid. Didn't I mean anything to you?"

"Oh baby," Phee moved towards her daughter.

"Remember, she can neither feel nor hear you. You are dead to her."

"It wasn't my fault that I wasn't there for you. No one would let me see you. They took you away from me. It wasn't my fault," Phee was crying, too.

"Wasn't it?" asked Jinn. "Who gave up? Who wasn't around to fight for her? Come."

And, with that, they were back in Phee's hospital room. "Think, Phee. Your life isn't just about you. Everyone in the course of his or her life touches many other people. Our lives have an impact far beyond ourselves. Next time, you will see more of the many others. Now rest."

Chapter 30

Devon, back at his apartment, heard his phone playing the dwarf song from *The Hobbit*. He saw he had a text from Garret. In fact, he had several.

-garret981 ->devonwrtr

Not trying to bug you. Coffee, remember?

Shit! Devon quickly texted Garret that there'd been a problem at the gallery and he had been at the hospital the past day and a half. Could they meet now? He did want to see him.

Fifteen minutes later, Garret arrived at the coffee shop down the block and saw Devon sitting there scowling at his phone.

"Hey."

"Hey. Been a hell of a few days. One of my friends tried to commit suicide, other stuff."

"No problem, together now. Coffee. Finished your book. It was awesome. Got such a kick out of the cat all the way through the book. Great ending, loved the Salerian getting the shit kicked out of him finally, and that Jehara did it."

"Thanks," Devon grinned. "Jehara is the main character in the next book."

"Sweet."

"Did you say you had a cat the other night?" Garret asked.

"Love cats. Can't have one where I live, or I would have one."

"Want to go see Hemingway?"

Garret grinned. "Yes."

Chapter 31

Peter lay in bed trying to wrap his mind around his son not being his son any more. Hospitals, he decided, were not a good place to try and think about anything of any importance. Monitors buzzed and beeped, intercoms blared for Dr. So-and-so to go to wherever and nurses had the annoying habit of interrupting at the worst possible moment. Lab techs came in to poke him on a regular basis, the respiratory therapist came through to make sure he was still breathing, and chipper old ladies dressed in grey stripes came through to ask him oh-so-cheerfully if there was anything they could do for him.

All he wanted was to be left alone. *His son's name was Piper? What kind of a name was that? Good glass artist, though. Had to give him ... her* (he shuddered causing the machine to chirp/beep faster) *credit there. Phenomenal, actually. Real talent. No question.*

The real question was: could he accept Peter, ah, Piper (BEEP!) *and if not, was he willing to walk away from his...kid?* (BEEPBEEP-CHIRP!)

The day nurse came into his room. "Mr. McAllister, are you okay, sir? You in pain, need some medication? It is almost time…"

"No, I'm fine," he groused at the interruption.

"Well, just let me know if there's a problem."

He nodded. *You are the problem,* he thought. *Go. Away. Where was he? He wanted to walk away. He shook his head. No, no matter if he didn't understand, disagreed with the entire concept, thought the whole thing was utterly stupid, he could not just walk away. He didn't want to lose, hell, to lose either of them. But Peter had been his son. Sons were special. They were the real descendants, the continuation of the name, the line, the family. A daughter would be a descendant too, but no matter what the doctors could do surgically to make Peter a female, there wouldn't be any children. Couldn't be.*

That was part of what was killing him. The line had been drawn in the sand. No more McAllisters, no blood McAllisters, anyway. That, in a strange way, really hurt, left him with a hollow space deep within his being.

He didn't like the feeling one bit. The last time he had felt this way had been when Laura…when Laura had disappeared on him. She had been the one that the movies raved about, the other half of his soul, the everything that he could ever want. Sure, her family had money and his hadn't. Sure, she was from a far higher branch of the social tree, but he thought that hadn't mattered; they loved each other. Then, she was gone. He looked, called, wrote…cried. She had vanished as if she had never been born. It had taken him years to get over her. And, indeed, he'd found another.

But while it was very special, it wasn't the same and it never had the chance to grow into what it might have been. His wife died giving birth, and that was it.

It had always been the two of them; a man and his son. Now, Peter was gone as well. Could he accept Piper, love Piper? He tried get his mind to exchange one for the other. It was incredibly difficult. Yet… yet he wanted his child to be happy, healthy, whole. He really had nothing to choose between, because the only choices he had were to accept Piper or walk away. They hadn't been at all close the last five years and he had really missed knowing Peter. Now he understood why it had been that way. His child needed the time to become who he was. And his child had done it alone, understanding that the parent would have fought tooth and nail to keep everything as it had been.

He shook his head. He had to admit that doing this alone had taken guts, determination and courage. How could he fault that? Short answer, he couldn't. Pure and simple.

Thinking on it some more, Peter McAllister realized that he didn't need to agree as much as accept. It really wasn't his life that had changed, just the semantics. *Rock meet hard place*, he thought. *Man up*, he told himself and then laughed at the phrase. Piper proved without a doubt that strength or fortitude weren't male traits.

Feeling somewhat like a little kid in school, Peter considered that there would be much he needed to rethink. *Piper would need to be patient too*, he mused. *They would have to walk this path together, even if he did have to run a little to catch up.*

A knock at the door had him looking up to see Dr. Daniels standing in the doorway.

"Safe to come in?" he asked, smiling.

"Yes, it is," answered Peter. "You gave me a lot to think about last time. Couldn't have been easy for you, given that I didn't want to hear any of it."

"Understandable. News like that is a shock under the best of conditions. So have you come to any conclusions?"

He nodded. "I might have taken the long way through the thought process, but yes, I have. I want to see Piper." He tested the words out loud for the first, accepting time. I'd like to see my daughter."

Chapter 32

Piper clicked off her phone call with her father's doctor. Her dad was doing much better and he wanted to see her. *Her.* Not Peter. Piper.

She looked in her closet. What should she wear? She wanted to look just right. Piper had heard Devon come in a while ago. Without thinking, she went across the hall and knocked on his door. If he was writing, oh well. She needed his help. When he didn't answer right away, she banged again.

"Hang on a second!" She heard him yell and impatiently walked in a circle.

"Hurry up!" she hollered back.

"I'm coming, I'm coming, geez." Devon opened the door still zipping his jeans. "What?"

She just looked at him. "Sorry, but I__" she broke off see-ing another man walking out of the bedroom, buttoning his shirt. "Oh. I ah…"

Shaking his head and grinning, he said, "Well, c'mon in. Piper, this is Garret. Garret, Piper."

Hemingway strolled up to Piper, purring madly. Grateful for the break, Piper leaned over and ran a hand the length of the cat's back and tail.

"Hi," Piper hurried the greeting. "Devon, I need your help. Now."

"What's up?"

"Dad's doctor called and Dad wants to see me, to talk to me. He's okay with my being me. That sounds funny, but you understand, right?"

"Yeah, I do. SO what do you need help with?"

"I don't know what to wear," she wailed. "It's got to be just right."

"It's not like you are going to a job interview or anything, Pipe."

"But..."

"C'mon, Garret, let's go invade the lady's closet."

Somewhat bemused, Garret followed Piper, Devon and the cat next door. Devon stuck his head in her closet and rifled through her clothes. "Oh, we do need to take you shopping. Okay, skirt, dress or pants?"

"Dress or skirt, I think. Kind of a statement, you know?"

"Okay," he grabbed a long flowing three tiered skirt, a wide leather belt and a soft muslin green blouse and tossed them to her. You have boots, right? Those," he said pointing. "Perfect. Now go put them on," he said pointing to the bathroom. "Okay if I fill Garret in on what's going on?"

He took her muffled answer as permission and told Garret about Piper, her dad and the recent revelations. When she came out of the bathroom five minutes later, both of the men grinned.

"Yes. Feminine, but not showy," Devon pronounced. "Perfect for a first meeting with the dad you've had your whole life."

"You sure?"

"Absolutely."

"God, I am so nervous, Dev."

"Just be you. You'll be fine. Remember you are the 'phenomenal new glass artist who stretches the boundaries' and who 'is enchanting the art world!'"

"Huh?"

"Haven't you read your reviews, darling? You are the rage. You've arrived! In more ways than one, I might add."

"Really?" she squealed. "With everything going on, I hadn't even thought about it!"

"I've got them all next door. You were a mega hit across the board! So was Cee. You both rocked it!"

"Still."

"Sweetie, a wise woman once told me that if you go in thinking you've lost, then the other person or the battle to come is already lost before the first salvo is ever fired. You know who you are. Now go show him his fantastic daughter!"

"Okay. I can do this. I hope. I'm," she hesitated, "sorry if I interrupted anything."

"Nah," smiled Garret, "I just came over to meet the cat."

"Uh huh, sure you did," she grinned. "New euphemism, eh?"

"Worked for us," laughed Devon.

Chapter 33

Jinn was sprawled in the chair next to Phee's bed. "Bout time you woke up," she said.

"Oh God. You again?"

"Yup. Ready for another trip?"

"No, not really," Phee replied. "I'm still upset from the last one."

"Get over it. Let's go." Jinn took Phee by the hand, and suddenly they were in Piper's apartment.

Piper and Devon were sharing a two-thirds empty bottle of Jameson's. Piper'd been crying. Devon looked as if he were barely conscious. Three shot glasses were on the table. One was full, the other two empty.

Piper poured out two more shots. "Here's to the rooms full of faux fur Phee had," she said raising her glass.

Clicking his glass to hers, Devon slurred, "Try sayin' that three times fast," he grinned before downing the shot.

Refilling the glasses again, Devon said, "Here's to the woman she should have been, could have been."

Piper slammed her empty glass down on the table. "Such a damn shame. I wish she'd told me. I kind of had a clue, but I wasn't sure. It isn't like you can go up to someone and say, 'Oh, by the way, are you trans?' you know?"

Devon laughed. "No, you really can't do that. Imagine if she hadn't been!" He poured two more shots.

"I wish I'd had a chance to get to know her better. Her being a model and all was so very cool."

"She could have been such a role model for so many people." They drank.

"Bad pun, Dev," said Piper giggling. "But very true."

"Right," Phee said to Jinn sarcastically. "Me a role model."

"You could be. Do you know that there's a four page spread in Vogue this month by a transgender model named Andreja Pejic? She's not only wedged open the door in transgender modeling and general acceptance, she's kicked it in! Why should you be any different? Everyone starts somewhere, you know."

Refilling the glasses with the last drops in the bottle of Jameson's, Piper said, "Here's to people being true to themselves, to being brave enough to take on the world and being strong enough to kick some ass!"

Downing the last shot, she looked over at Devon, who was passed out cold with Hemingway on his stomach. Hemingway's pink tongue was inching towards Devon's glass.

Piper grinned, picked up first Devon's glass and then the full shot that had been on the table the whole time. With the full shot still in her hand, she said, "Here's to the Phoenix!" and drank most of it down before dropping it on the floor and falling asleep in her chair.

Hemingway hopped down, sniffed at the fallen glass, sneezed and, turning around three times, settled in to sleep as well. "You could have had some really good friends in those two, if you'd given them half a chance," Jinn said as the walls shifted around them.

Now they were in Timiny's studio. Timiny was watching a spiky-haired model do her runway walk for him wearing one of his creations. Both Jinn and Phee could hear his thoughts.

Not good. No flair. God, she swishes. Not what I want at all.

Damn Phee anyway. No one wears my creations like she did. Damn it all, I need her.

Walls dissolved again. Now they were in an apartment that was unfamiliar to Phee.

"Who's that?" she said, pointing at the woman seated on a window seat looking out a drizzle-patterned window at the rain. They couldn't see her face, only a blurred image reflected in the window.

"She must remain nameless. She knows she is missing that one person who can make her life complete, but she hasn't been able to find her. Then again, she never will, now, because the woman she was supposed to meet and fall in love with killed herself before she ever had a chance to meet her. She's been wanting to meet another transgender like herself, someone who really will pick up all the nuances in thought and conversation that straight people can't, probably won't, ever truly understand. She's seriously considering her alternatives, and, at the moment, she is very depressed. She has so much love to give, and she's feeling like there is no one out there who wants it."

The setting changed. "Wait! Let me see her face," begged Phee. "No."

Now they were in Phee's apartment. Her mother and sister were sorting through Phee's things. "Remember this?" her mom asked, holding up —"

The scene froze as Phee rounded on Jinn. "I want to go back to the other scene, the one where the woman was. I need to know who she is. Take me back there!" she insisted.

And they were instantly back in Phee's hospital room. Jinn looked at Phee and slowly shook her head. "Some things are not permitted. I think you've seen enough for today. Rest and think about what you've seen and heard."

"But I don't want to…"

Jinn floated above Phee. She thought that just perhaps, she was beginning to get through to Phee. Perhaps. Time would tell. It always did.

Chapter 34

Piper stood in the doorway to her father's hospital room. She saw that he was looking at his laptop, reading something on the screen. She rapped softly on the doorjamb and he looked over and smiled.

"Hey, Dad."

"Come here. I never really got a good look at you the other night before ... before everything happened. You are beautiful."

"Thanks, Dad. You are looking pretty good for someone who just had surgery, yourself." Standing awkwardly next to his bed, she hesitated for a minute and then asked, "Can I have a hug?"

At his nod, she bent over and hugged her father for the first time in years. "I've missed that, Dad."

"I have too. Can I ask you something?"

"Sure."

"Why 'Piper?' Why did you pick that name?"

"Remember when I was a little kid and the kids would tease me, calling me 'Peter Piper' and how much I hated that? Well, when I was going through transition, before I had the surgery, I decided that I would own that and never let it bother me again. I became Piper and I've never looked back since."

"Piper. I like it. It fits you," he said with a smile that, this time, reached his eyes, and she could see that it did.

"I didn't think there was any chance of your being at the opening. I thought you were on the east coast. I would have let you know..." she paused. "I wouldn't have had you find out the way you did."

"I only decided to come at the last minute. Joshua, the gallery owner, was so insistent. Did he know, does he know about you and that we are related?"

"I don't think so, at least until then I don't think he had a clue. Bios about you mention a son," she smiled, "not a daughter."

"True. Sit," he said. "I want to show you the article that I posted before you got here. It will be in the paper tomorrow. I hope you are okay with it. I wrote two. One covers The Gallery opening and talks about the work of all the artists, yours included. I wrote it from my notes before, well, before everything. Your work is brilliant. You've done things with glass that I never knew could be done. You should be very proud of yourself. I know I am."

Piper's face went from pleased to happy to total tears.

"What? What did I say wrong?" Monitors beeped frantically, but neither heard them.

"N-nothing. I am so happy. You truly mean that? About my work and being proud of me?"

"I do."

"Oh Dad," she sniffed. "Nothing could mean any more to me than that."

"I don't guess I've been all that supportive of you in the past. I figure if you can start a new life as Piper, I get to start a new one as Piper's dad."

She reached in her purse for some tissues, and handed one to her father as well. "Deal."

"Now, read the article."

On The Other Side of the Glass
I've been an art critic for thirty years. I

have the reputation of being hard, difficult and not one who easily gives praise. I was at an opening at 'The Gallery' Saturday night. (see side article from notes written earlier in the evening before I 'met' the glass artist.)

It had been a memorable evening, as seeing the collective work of the four featured artists was an art critic's dream. All four, each in their own ways, were inspiring and creative, executing their various art forms well. One artist in particular (as evidenced by my notes) quite literally blew me away. Being who I am (or I should say 'have been') I usually do what is oft- termed 'damning with faint praise.' I give with one hand and then take away with the other.

The creations of glass artist, Piper McAllister, of Pipedreams Studio, were a cut above everything I have seen. From her incredible hanging chandelier in the atrium to her smaller pieces, I found a variety of nuance rarely seen. I couldn't wait to meet the artist.

When I did, I received the shock of my life. At first, it was if I were seeing a blurred image, as if I were looking through a thick piece of a ntique glass, the sort that makes everything wavy and indistinct.

The woman looked like my son. I was thinking that it couldn't be he... And, then I had the heart attack that (according to my doctor) saved my life. After a few days of adjusting, days that included having open-heart surgery and a (no pun intended) heart to heart conversation with my doctor, I realized a few things I'd like to share with you now.

138

First of all, I have always been one of those men who was inordinately proud, peacock proud, of having a son and all that it implied (in an old-fashioned sense). Finding that I had a trans-gender child was like hitting a very solid brick wall. My glass heart shattered.

Second, I have always been, shall we say, implacable. My way or the highway, I'm the dad, what I say not only goes, but is. Make that all caps —what I say IS!

Third, I have to admit that I was wrong — was I ever wrong — on so many levels, in so many ways. I spent these past few days of adjustment thinking about my child's life. I thought about many things, both things that mattered, and things that, in the larger scheme of things, really didn't. I realized that, as much as I initially thought it was, what was important wasn't something about me. It was about my kid being able to be whole, healthy and happy. As overwhelming as my son's decision initially seemed, I had nothing much to do with it. Well, not much except for being the sort of parent who was so condescending, close-minded and selfish that my child had been forced to go out and do this entirely on his, (scratch that!)her own without the support of the one person that was supposed to be there for his kid come hell or high water. More, my kid was abso-lutely right to do it alone, because before the fact, I never would have understood or wanted to understand — let alone accept that my kid had known all along what was right.

I'd like to introduce my daughter to the world. World, meet Miss Piper McAllister. She's a glass artist extraordinaire and one heck of an awesome woman. I am so very proud of her.

Lastly, I'll share one more thing. She is coming to visit me today. It will be the first time I have seen her in several years. I am one very excited and lucky dad. If I weren't stuck in a hospital bed, I'd be out buying pink ribbons and handing out cigars. I haven't seen her yet, you see, but by the time you read this, she will have read it, and I hope, be proud of her old man.

"Oh Dad, I love you!"

"I wasn't sure how you felt about people knowing one way or the other. I can change that part, if you want me to."

"Don't change a single word. Thank you. Right now, I'm pretty damned proud of you as well!" Piper sat and scooted close to her father and gave him a long (gentle) hug.

Dr. Daniels, who'd been quietly standing in the doorway and who'd been totally unnoticed, stepped back into the hallway and walked to the nurses station smiling broadly.

Chapter 35

"Did you see these reviews?" squeaked Cee, holding up the latest ones.

"Sure did," said Galen. "Can't ask for much better than that! Even Peter McAllister! His reviews usually slam artists because he is always thinking they can do better or should be better or something. But he was very keen on your clock piece!"

"Sure should make The Gallery folks happy too. I need to go by there today and see when they will want more work brought by. I have some to bring in, but I need to know how much more he wants."

"See? And you were worrying that he'd want you to bring stuff home, silly you. I told you that you had nothing to worry about!"

When C.M. Baker walked through the doors into The Gallery, there were people everywhere. Heading straight upstairs to Josh's office, she was happy to see he was there.

"Ah, the esteemed C.M. Baker! Good, you brought me more work. How much more do you have? I need to talk to you about pricing. I think we can up your prices by a good thirty percent given the feedback I've gotten on your work.

Cee beamed. "This is all very exciting."

"I expect this will make you even happier, he said, handing her a check.

Her eyes widened as she looked at an amount that floored her. Trying her best to tamp down her excitement, she failed. She gave up and screamed instead.

"I take it that is a good scream?"

Eyes flooded, she nodded happily, not trusting herself to get out intelligible words.

"Good. Let me see what you've brought me," he said, reaching for the pieces she'd put on the table. "Oh, I like this one of the birds, and this and..." He just stared. Holding up the one she'd drawn of the chandelier hanging in the atrium, he said, "Oh. Not this one.Can't put this up for sale."

"Was there some sort of copyright infringement or something?" Her smile had vanished. She'd worked very hard on her interpretation of the sculpture.

"Hmm. No. What price did you have on this?" he mumbled, looking at the back. "Ah, nope. Sorry."

"Oh," she said, totally disappointed. "I'm sorry you don't want it."

"Didn't say that," he smiled. "I said I couldn't put it up for sale. Given your new pricing, minus The Gallery cut, I'll cut you a check for fifteen percent more than what's on here right now. Cee, this one is staying put in The Gallery. We are going to open a room of Permanent Exhibits. None of the pieces will be for sale; they will belong to The Gallery."

"Oh. Oh!" she repeated. "Wow. Okay. Whew! I thought you didn't like it or want it or something."

"Nope. Nothing further from the truth."

She sat, afraid her legs wouldn't support her if she continued standing. She took several deep breaths. "Okay, I'm okay now," she said smiling. "Have you seen the article about Mr. McAllister and Piper?

"I just finished reading it," he said. "I'm so pleased for

Piper." Suddenly, he understood what about Piper had puzzled him. "I'll be right back. I need to talk to Emily. Or if you could come back for your check?"

"Sure."

"Good," and Josh flew out the door.

I wonder what that was all about, she mused and then looked down at the check she still held in her hand.

Josh found Emily in the kitchen making sandwiches. "Emily! I figured out what it was about Piper that was driving me nuts! Kind of a little thing, given the article in the paper and all, but she looked so familiar to me because it was like looking at a female version of myself."

"I wondered when you'd get around to that," Em smiled. "I put that together a bit ago. Have you thought any more about what you are going to do?"

"I have to talk to him. I think maybe I need to visit him in the hospital, before he gets out and heads elsewhere. I need to know for sure, although I know inside he is my father. "I want the chance to really get to know him, Em – the way I know you and the girls."

She nodded. "I do too. Do you want me to go with you or is this something you need to do on your own?"

"I don't know. Let me think about it, okay?"

"Sure. Josh," she hugged him, "I'm okay either way. I have something else to tell you as well."

"What?"

"I spoke with Jinn. I was really wishing I had her to talk to the other day when you went on your wander to think. Suddenly, there she was."

He smiled. "Have you told Emma you talked to her ghostie?"

"Not yet, I will now, but I wanted to tell you first. And," she continued, "I kind of wanted to keep it just for me for a bit. Sound silly?"

"Of course not. She's your sister. Maybe she'll be able to

stick around a bit and you can have some of what you missed growing up."

"I'd really like that, but I'm not going to get my hopes up. I'll take whatever time we are given and be happy with that. It is so much more than the little I had. I'm grateful for it."

"I am too. Does she look like you or like we saw her in the hospital?"

"She looks like she did only without the bandages and bruises and such. She kind of glows, a sparkly, glow-y, see-through Jinn."

"I just saw a sparkly C.M. Baker downstairs. I thought she was going to faint when I gave her the check! Oh, and she brought more work in, including one she did of Piper's atrium piece. When I told her I wouldn't sell it, she looked awfully upset – until I told her that The Gallery would be buying it for a permanent display, as if it were an idea you and I had already discussed. Really, though, I thought of it just then."

"A permanent display of work? What a great idea! I love it, especially, because, as you know, artists come and stay for a bit then go elsewhere or something. You are so smart," she said hugging him. "Where?"

"Where what?"

"Where will the permanent display be? We thought we had so much room, but we are already running out."

"Ah. Hmm. I haven't gotten that far yet."

Chapter 36

Piper, Devon, Garret and the cat all were at Piper's apartment. The remnants of take-out Chinese littered her coffee table. "Time for fortune cookies!" Garret announced. Devon rolled his eyes, but picked a fortune cookie out of the pile, opened it and broke it open.

"'The dog may be wonderful prose, but only the cat is poetry,'" he read.

Both Garret and Devon cracked up laughing.

Garret picked out his. "'If we treated everyone we meet with the same affection we bestow upon our favorite cat, they, too, would purr.' - Martin Buxbaum."

Now they were laughing hysterically.

Piper picked up the last one and read it to herself. 'Give unto others that which you have taken.'

"What's yours say?" Devon asked. "Pipe?"

"Oh, here." She handed it to Devon and continued thinking. Devon and Garret read it. "What? Something's got you thinking."

"Just an idea I had earlier that this goes along with. Sort of. I think, maybe. Not sure, I need to think about it some more, first. How's Phee doing? Any change?"

"I heard from her mother that the EEG is showing more

activity. She says the doctor says that it is a very good sign."

"Hmm."

"What?"

"Just thinking. What the heck. You know I got a check from The Gallery today, right?"

"Yes, and …?"

"Well, it is for a lot of money. As in a *whole* lot. As in more money than I've ever seen written on a check. I was thinking, just for starters, that I'd give some to Stewie and get Phee's rent caught up and then, maybe…"

"Piper, you are driving me crazy! Maybe what?"

"Maybe, I could help out with her surgery."

"You made that much at the opening?"

Piper stood, got the check out of her wallet and then handed it to Devon. "Yes."

"Holy shit! I guess you did. Hey Gar, we know a rich and famous artist!"

"I don't know about famous," Piper demurred, "but I think maybe I'm rich. At least richer than I've ever been before. Josh says he's upping my prices by thirty percent, too."

Dev shook his head. "That is incredible, Piper. Phee'd freak."

"Yeah, she would. But Dev, if it hadn't been for my grandmother, I never could have had the surgery. So maybe, I'm supposed to help someone else get it. Kind of a pay it forward sort of thing."

"That'd be a wonderful thing to do," Garret said softly. "It's one of those things that never happens in real life, but would in a book or something. It's kind, immeasurably kind. We all get the 'being different' thing. We've lived it. Lived with the grief, the bullying, the teasing, the worry and the doubt. But for someone to give that kind of a gift, it's still mind-boggling."

Dev looked a little dazed. "Piper, not in any way to take away from your stupendous idea, but I've got some money tucked away from my last book. Would you mind if I added some to the pot?"

"She shook her head in disbelief. "That'd be great, Dev, but..."

"Ah Dev, although I don't know her, I sure know the problems," Garret spoke up. "If you and I are going to be together like we think, would you mind if I added some as well, as long as you wouldn't mind, Piper."

"The TFTFF! The Third Floor Transgender Female Fund!" marveled Devon.

"That's too complicated. How about The Phoenix Fund?" Piper suggested.

"Yes!" Devon agreed. "We could make up some official document that says that, once she's approved, she's getting it done!"

"I could do the art work for it," offered Garret. "Piper, could you make a glass Phoenix to hold it?"

"I can," she said, remembering her decision never to make any unicorns or the like. But this was different.

"Assuming she comes out of the coma," Devon said soberly.

Chapter 37

Piper was in her studio. She'd heated the gathering of glass several times, stretching, working the glass, but she hadn't been able to create the vision in her mind. She put it back in the fire until it become nothing more than a glob of molten glass again. Absently, she let the molten glass drip off the end of the pipe, the drops hitting her bucket of water. They sizzled for a moment as they cooled.

Laying the pipe aside, she waited a few minutes and lifted one of the drops from the water. A 'Prince Rupert's Tear' was what it was called. It was a simple thing – potentially a dangerous one if mishandled.

Looking like a teardrop with a tail, it was similar to a small tadpole and about the same size. The outer edges had cooled far faster than the internal body of the glass, and the process had created a tension in the body of the drop. You could take a hammer to the drop and nothing would happen, the hammer would bounce off the glass, not harming it in the least. Yet if one twisted the bit of a tail, it disintegrated from the tail to the body in a fraction of a second.

Thinking about that, she ran her finger over the round belly of the tear that rested in her palm. Wrapping several in cotton batting, she slipped them in her pocket and closed things down. Grabbing a couple pair of safety glasses and some gloves, she put them in a bag and went to see her father.

"Hi," she said from the doorway.

"Hi, yourself."

"I've been thinking," Piper began, "We've had our rough patches over the years, you and I. Some parts of it, I understand. Others I don't. We've never really discussed the problem areas before."

"No, we never have in any depth. I know I always shut you down."

She nodded. "I don't want us to do that anymore. I want us to be able to trust each other, trust in each other. Do you think we could try to do that?"

"I'd like it if we could, Piper. I expect it will be as hard for you to learn to trust in me as it will be for me to learn to trust in you. Trust and I have had our differences over the years, and I've sometimes been the loser. It is very hard for me to trust anyone or anything."

"I know," she said quietly. "I've always felt as if there were huge places you wouldn't let me near."

"There were. It was too difficult to open that whole ball of wax, especially for parts that had no answers. But I will try. Part of it goes back to before you were born and a woman named Laura, whom I loved beyond all reason and who I, for reasons I will never know, lost."

"Funny thing about trust, Dad. That whole 'two-way street' thing. I do understand though. Sometimes, it is so very difficult to trust. Harder still, to either rebuild lost trust or to trust again, even when the circumstances are different. I brought you something."

"You did?"

"Are you allowed to go outside?"

"I might be able to escape the keepers of the zoo. Where are we going?"

"Just outside, away from any other people. It's warm out there."

Her father stood up from the chair where he'd been sitting and sat down in his wheelchair (which had deliberately been placed close by) instead. He took a piece of paper from his notebook and scribbled a note in case anyone came looking for him: 'I'm outside with my daughter.'

"Let's go before anyone stops us," he said.

Outside in the courtyard, their having gone as far as she could push him in the chair, Piper sat on a stone wall by some low plantings.

She put her hand in her pocket and took out one of the wrapped Prince Rupert tears. Unraveling the cotton, she placed the tear in the palm of her hand, explaining to her father what it was and how it was made.

"I've cried for us, Dad. I've cried for you and for me. A few years back, I decided I wasn't going to cry any more. We are family, Dad. We talked about trust back in your room. Trust can form a formidable barrier against the world."

She put the tear down on the stonewall with the thin fragile tip up in the air. Picking up a stone, she hit the main part of the tear as hard as she could. The rock bounced off. "See, Dad? Here, the body is strong. You can't break it. Put these on."

She handed him a pair of safety glasses and the gloves. She put on her own as well. "Trust can also be extremely fragile. A careless word or action can destroy it."

Piper twisted the tip of the tail and the entire tear shattered as if it had never been. All that was left was a bit of dust.

"What...what did you do? WHY..." her father was visibly startled.

"Let's be careful with our tears and our trust, okay?" Piper said by way of explanation. "It is too important. You are important to me. I don't want to lose you again. I want you in my life. I want to be in yours."

Peter McAllister nodded. "A long time ago, I dreamed about having a large family – a family I could see in generations. Grand-children. Being a grandfather. But, sometimes what we get is different from what we thought we always wanted and we realize that dreams can change. We need to accept that and go forward to whatever comes next."

A single tear rolled down his cheek. Piper caught it with her finger. "I know we said things, good things, the other day. But I need to ask you this. Can you really love me as Piper? All the way, a hundred percent, 'daddy's little girl' love me?"

He nodded, far too moved for words.

Chapter 38

Phee woke to see Jinn tracing the heart monitor's lines with her index finder. Up, down, up, down.

"What are you doing?" Phee asked grumpily.

"Watching your heart beat. You have a very strong heart, more, a big heart. Why are you lying in a hospital bed? You should be out in the fresh air, living, modeling, planting flowers, some-thing—anything but lying here with a super case of oh-poor-me-itis. There are people here who want more to live than anything, who will die today. They don't have a choice. They have not given up, nor do they want to. They would rather live than die – even if it is living with only one leg, incredible pain or knowing their days are severely numbered.

"Suicide hurts everyone that is left behind. They can't grieve honestly, because they blame themselves and think the death is on them, when it is not. If you were to ask someone, anyone, 'should I kill myself,' every person would tell you 'no' and give you bunches of reasons why you should not. They could also give you many reasons why you or anyone should choose to live.

"Most importantly, Phee, you have so much to give, to do, to BE! Sure, there might be hard times. We all go through that. We grouse, grumble, complain and then do what needs doing to fix the problem."

"How did you die?"

"My parachute didn't open. Some people used to say that I had a death wish because I was an adrenaline junkie and took extreme chances. I did take some calculated chances and made some *really* stupid choices, but I had no desire to die that day nor any other. My life wasn't perfect. I had problems and issues, just like everyone else. But, whether I wanted to or not, I did die. Now I'm trapped behind this window and I can come and try to help you or others, but I'm not alive. I can't do whatever I want. I have rules and obligations just as anyone does. Worse, I can't get a hug or feel a human touch. And I can't stay, when it is what I want to do more than anything else.

"Come."

In that one word, Jinn and Phee were at Phee's tenth high school reunion. "What are we doing here?" Phee asked. "I'd never come to this!"

"That's why we are here. Listen."

"Hey, did you know that Bob was transgender?" A tall willowy blond was talking to Danny, the overweight guy who used to be the captain of the football team.

"Seriously? Very cool. I always wondered about him."

"Wondered what?" she asked.

"Well, I knew he always felt that he couldn't quite fit in, I didn't know why, but he clearly didn't. Got to give him, or I should say her, a lot of credit. Don't know as I would have the guts, no matter how I felt inside."

"Guess she didn't have as much guts as you thought. She killed herself a couple of months ago."

"That's terrible!" he said, shocked. "Wasn't she a model or wanting to be?"

"That's what I heard. Kind of pisses me off, too. The woman 'Bob' had a chance to be such a role model. Saw a picture of her. She was beautiful. I remember wishing I were as pretty as she was."

"Well, you are prettier than she is now. You are still here."

"That's mean," pouted Phee to Jinn.

"No, it is honest. Look over there. Do you remember Jimmy?"

"Yeah, quiet kid. A nerd."

"He's transgender too," Jinn said. "He just heard that you killed yourself. He always idolized you. Did you know that?"

"No, I hung with a different group."

"He is thinking that if you couldn't deal with life as a transgender, that there's no way he can."

"That's not true!" Phee spun around to face Jinn, protesting. "Jimmy's really smart and, even if he was a geek, he was a nice one. He isn't thinking about committing suicide, is he?"

"He is now."

"You can't lay that on me! That's not fair."

"Truth rarely is," Jinn spoke steadily. What we do affects others. Choices we make ripple out, intersect with other people's rippled choices. Every time those ripples coincide, choices, feelings, habits, words: all can be affected. People do, indeed, die alone, but their death is never isolated, affecting no one. The ripples reach out infinitely. Phee, we live and breathe connected. What one person chooses to do today can have an impact on someone else years later. This is one of the things I've had to realize, to learn. It is one of the reasons I am here and not inside the mansion yet. It is so much better to live well, to make positive choices."

"Yeah, well, the landlord shouldn't have tried to evict me. That was like the last straw."

"Perhaps he shouldn't," Jinn nodded. "But, did you bother to take the steps available that could have helped?"

"What about my ex stopping me from seeing my daughter? Are you going to try to tell me there was something I could have done about that?"

Jinn nodded. "It might take time, but there is always something that can be done, even if that 'thing' is just giving time a chance. Taking your life cuts that thread forever. Fine. No 'somethings' then. You are dead. But what about your daughter having to live with that? Is that fair to her?"

They were back in Phee's room. Her monitors were all beeping, alarms were going off and blue lights were flashing in the hallway. People were (although the scene seemed to progress in slow motion) about to rush into Phee's room.

"Choose. Phee, you need to choose. Now. You have been given an incredible gift, a second chance. You must choose to live or die. You can choose life and make it the best life you possibly can, muddling through both the good and the bad but always giving it your best. You can choose to be a force to be reckoned with, whether it's a role model or just a normal person fighting for what you believe is possible.

"Or you can choose to die. No more chances. I hope you make the right choice, Phoenix. Remember why you chose 'Phoenix' to be your new name.

"I have said and done all I can to help you. It is up to you. Will the Phoenix fly or fall into the ashes?" And Jinn was gone.

Chapter 39

Emma woke up completely, even though she'd been asleep for quite a while.

"Hi," Jinn said softly.

"You came back, again," Emma said, happily. "I wish you could stay all the time. Mommy really misses you. I'm glad you talked to her. I overheard Mommy and Daddy talking about you."

"I wish I could too, but I can't. You understand that, don't you?" Emma nodded. "You really shouldn't eavesdrop when your parents are having grown-up conversations, you know."

"I know, but it is the best way to find out things they think I'm too little to understand. You made Mommy really happy the other day."

"I'm glad I could do that, little one. I want you to know something. I love you so much. Please don't ever forget that. I love you all."

"You sound like you are going away."

"I will be very soon. I don't want to, but I have to follow the rules."

"Are you going to go help someone else?"

"Maybe. I don't know yet."

"If you are all done helping people, will you get to be in

heaven and have your wings and fly all over?"

Jinn smiled. "That would be fun. I'd rather be here with all of you, though."

Emma smiled. "But you can't. Rules are rules. Do you have bedtimes in Heaven?"

"I don't know. Maybe."

"You can't tell me too much can you?" Emma asked wisely.

"No," Jinn grinned. "I can't and aren't you a smart little monkey to figure that out."

"I told you, I'm smarter than people think. I guess it is good that we can't know too much about Heaven; otherwise people would want to go there before they should. I like being here where we are now. We went to the zoo! They don't have zoos there, do they?"

Jinn shook her head. "No cages in Heaven."

"I'm really sleepy. I love you, Auntie Jinn," Emma yawned.

"I love you, too. Bunches and bunches. I promise, I will come say goodbye."

But Emma was already asleep.

Chapter 40

Emily stood in the office doorway. "Josh, I had an idea. Why don't you bring your book to Peter McAllister and ask him to sign it?"

"He'd see inside it then," Josh objected, "He'd see what Mom wrote. She wrote, 'From your mother, Laura.' "

"I know," Emily smiled. "Perhaps it will make it easier to ask what you want to ask."

"It might at that," Josh mused. "I thought maybe I'd go over to the hospital today."

"Probably be a good idea. Don't expect he'll be in there too much longer. Hmm. Wonder who's at the door? Not used to the doorbell yet." Emily walked over and opened their front door to see Piper standing there.

"Hi Piper, come in."

"Is Joshua here? I went to The Gallery's doors, but it isn't open yet."

"Yes, he is. We're in the kitchen having our 'the kids are gone to school' morning coffee recovery time," she smiled.

"I'd have waited until The Gallery was open, but I really need to talk to him now."

"Okay. It isn't a problem." Emily walked her to the kitchen. "I'll leave you two to talk."

"No, please stay," Piper said. "I should probably talk to both of you."

Emily poured Piper some coffee and motioned her to a chair. Piper was staring at Joshua.

"What? Did I grow horns or something?"

"N-no. I need to ask you a weird question. Did you have a Grandmother Alice?"

Emily hissed in a breath. Josh's eyes widened. "We, Em and I, both did. Why?"

"So did I. Well, she wasn't my blood grandmother, but sort of a slant-wise one. I never met her, but she left me some money years ago after she died. My dad and I didn't have any idea who she was or anything. The lawyers wouldn't tell us anything either. Then this was delivered by a messenger this morning." She pointed to the envelope she'd put on the table.

"According to the first letter inside this, the lawyers had been trying to find me for about five years. Dad and I had moved and then I was overseas until just recently. It didn't help," she continued, looking at them shyly, "that my name changed. When The Gallery opened, they were able to find me."

"What's in the letter, Piper?" asked Emily gently.

"Josh, what was your mother's name?"

"Laura. Her name was Laura."

Piper took a deep breath. "Grandmother Alice said, in her letter, that my father and your mother were in love, but that something happened. She didn't know what, but that from what she learned, your mother was pregnant with you when she married your step-dad."

Josh nodded. "I found that out from Grandmother Alice as well, after she died and after both my step-father and then my mother had both passed away."

Emily looked from Piper to Joshua. All three of them stared at one another, and then all began talking at once.

"Then we are—"

"Then you are—"

"Then he is—"

They all stopped talking. Joshua and Piper just sat there looking at each other. "Okay," Emily began, as it was apparent she was the only one capable of talking at the moment. "So this means you and Piper are half brother and sister and that Peter McAllister is your father."

Emily pushed the art book towards Piper. "Look."

"My dad wrote this a long time ago." She opened the front cover and read what was written there. She looked up at Joshua. "Do you think she was hoping you'd figure it out someday?"

"Remember when I kept thinking I knew you?" Joshua turned to the back of the book, showing Piper the inner flap of the dust jacket. She looked at the thirty-some year old picture of her dad and then over to Josh.

"Wow. You didn't talk to my dad at the opening?"

"I was so busy running from place to place. I was coming up to him, when he saw you. Things were a bit crazy after that. I saw him when he was with the EMTs, but I didn't make the connection." He took Emily's hand, looking at his wife. "Em did."

"I didn't say anything for a day or so, then I asked Josh to go dig this book out. Do you know, this book was instrumental in Josh getting into both painting and then The Gallery. I had him look at the back page. He hadn't had the book out in years, but it was important enough that when he left home, it was one of the few items he took with him."

"Dad mentioned his Laura yesterday. He'd never mentioned her before, but he loved her. That was very clear."

"I don't supposed we will ever know the whole story. At least on my end," Josh said ruefully, "it was buried under layers of lies."

Josh grinned at Piper. "Well, Sis...can I have a hug?"

Piper stood. "I've always been an only child. Grandmother Alice gave me a whole family!" Tears streamed and all three of them ended up in a massive, and years overdue, hug.

Finally, swiping her hand across her eyes, Piper sniffed. "Emily, you said that Grandmother Alice was your grandmother too? Your little girl's name is Alice, isn't it."

Em nodded. "Josh's step-father and my mother were brother and sister although we didn't know it until after Grandmother Alice had passed away. We never met each other until quite a while later, and then by accident. I had a twin whom Josh had seen, but none of us knew about the various relationships until we were adults and received journals from our mutual grand-mother. The pieces, finally, all fit together. Somehow, I just know Grandmother Alice is smiling today."

"All her convoluted journals did what she meant for them to do; bring a family together." Josh looked over at his wife. She had a funny look on her face. "I know, hon, you wish Jinn were here."

"She is."

"That explains it." At Piper's confused look, Josh explained. "There is still a lot of the story you don't know, but now we will have all the time in the world to share it with you."

"Hmm." Piper took a sip of her cold coffee. "Are you going to go over to the hospital before Dad gets out today or..."

"I had planned to even though I wasn't a hundred percent sure he was who we thought he was. When you arrived, we were discussing how to bring the whole thing up. Not like I could walk in and say, 'Hi, I'm your son!' That would be a shocker even if he hadn't just had a heart attack."

"Yeah," Piper laughed. "From looking over and seeing your son is now your daughter!" Piper paused. "It's so nice to be able to laugh at something I was terrified of his finding out before I was ready to tell him, and then after how he did find out."

"What time are they cutting him loose?"

"I need to pick him up in," she checked her watch, "about fifteen minutes. He's going to be staying at The Broken Goose for a couple of weeks. They have a fitness center there, so it is perfect. I hired a nurse slash rehab lady to take care of him. She's half line-backer, half 'Atilla the Hun' and a total sweetheart. She'll be staying there as well. Happily, I could book the two rooms for the duration. Emily, you do understand I had to see you guys first? I couldn't go see him knowing…"

"Of course. Maybe you could bring him here? Say there is something you need to show him at The Gallery?"

"Good idea. But I think back here might be better."

"Yes," Emily agreed. "Here. In private."

They left, and Emily went out to the back deck. "Still here?"

Jinn shimmered. "Yes. So you will all be together soon."

"I wish you were here. I mean really here."

"I know. I do too. I keep thinking about all those journals she wrote. Do you think she ever imagined how it would all finally work out?"

"I think she hoped it would. Jinn? Can you find her, let her know?"

"I have no idea. I can try. I have a feeling she knows already. I can't explain it, but it's a feeling.

"You know, Emily, it is almost time for me to go."

Emily nodded. "You'll say goodbye? And you'll tell Emma?"

"Yes. I already promised Emma I would. She overhears a lot. She knew you and I had talked. It made her very happy. She's going to be thrilled to have a new grandpa. She told me she wants a "grampa." Her excitement will ease things for the other two as well."

"Do you know everything that's going on?"

Jinn shook her head. "Just some things, and even then, I don't always know why. I didn't know she'd actually be getting a 'grampa' for sure or how it would happen or who it would be. Sometimes, things just work out exactly as they are supposed to, I guess."

"Sometimes they kinda don't. But I am so happy we had this time."

"Me too. I need to go and you have company coming!"

Chapter 41

Phee tried to open her eyes, but they felt very heavy. She heard something beeping. "Phee, wake up now. C'mon Phee, wake up."

"Trying," she mumbled through cotton fuzz. "Thirsty."

She felt a straw touch her lips. Cool water soothed. She tried again and this time, successfully opened her eyes.

"What's going on. Where am I?" Her eyes darted around the room, latched on to those of her mother. "Mom? What happened?"

"You tell us." Phee moved her head and saw Dr. Schedley.

"I was in my apartment, taking a bath. I think I had too much to drink. I was kind of upset and took some valium. I must have passed out."

"If I might ask your mom and sister to leave for a few minutes?" her doctor requested. The two women stepped to the door.

"Phee, you've been in a coma since Saturday. It's Thursday."

"A coma? Shit. Oh my god! You think I tried... no way! Are you kidding me? No way in bloody hell! I'm too close to getting... oh no," she looked over at the doctor. "Please, please don't tell me this will mess up my getting the surgery done?"

"That depends on you."

"Damn. I was pissed about getting evicted and my stupid ex stopping me from seeing Chloe, but kill myself? I couldn't do that to her. She's my kid. I couldn't do that to me! After all I've been through to get this far? Hell no! I just got drunk. I was feeling sorry for myself. But not that sorry! Yeah, the valium was stupid. You do some stupid things when you are drunk and geez, it's been years. I don't even like being drunk. I hate hangovers. I am so thirsty," she said, struggling to sit up and drink more water.

"How much valium did you take?"

"Five. It lets me sleep." She rolled her eyes. Shook her head and immediately winced. "I had a bottle full. There was most of a prescription there. I wasn't trying to kill myself. Look in my journal."

"I did. You weren't sounding all that happy."

"I don't think I was sounding suicidal either. I was pissed."

"That may well be. Phee, due to the circumstances of your arrival here, I need to tell you that you will be here for thirty days--"

"I can't! I need to find a job so I don't lose my place."

"I'm sorry. State law. We'll continue the rest of your counseling sessions while you are here. If all goes well, by the time you get out things can progress from there."

Tears trickled down her cheeks. "I didn't try to kill myself."

"I'm inclined to agree with you. Let's make the best of the situation, okay? Again, there is no getting around it. We can check into some things to see if we can get your eviction postponed. Maybe your mother can help there. The important thing is that you are okay. It was iffy there for a bit. You know the statistics, Phee. I'm just very glad you didn't become one. I'll go tell your mom she can come back in. Talk to her and I'll stop by later."

Something buzzed in the back of Phee's mind, but it was too fuzzy. She felt as if she should be remembering something, but she couldn't quite grab onto it.

"Phee, sweetie. We were so worried about you."

164

"I'm okay, Mom. In a mess here, but I'm okay. I know how it looks, but I didn't try—"

"I know dear. You'll get through this. Do you want me to go to your apartment and bring you some jammies or sweats?"

Phee looked down at the papery gown she was wearing. "Please. And my toothbrush. My mouth feels like the alley behind the apartment."

Her sister went into the bathroom and returned with a toothbrush, toothpaste and a glass of water. "Here ya go, Sis. This'll help temporarily. You probably don't have your sea legs," she grinned.

Phee garbled a response through a mouthful of toothpaste, spat. "Oh that's better. Mom, I'm sorry. I can't imagine what you've been going through. I am so sorry. Forgive me?"

Her mother bent over and gave Phee a hug. "I love you."

The doctor said I should mention something to you. I really, really hate to ask, but if I'm stuck in here for another few weeks, is there any way you could help me out with my rent? I'll get kicked out if I don't get them money ASAP. I'll pay you back, I promise."

"Actually, you don't need to worry about that. I ran into your friends Piper and Devon. Piper's father ended up here the same night you did. He had a heart attack, but he's going to be okay. Piper and Devon talked to the landlord and you are paid up: all your back rent and for the next two months. He tore up the eviction papers."

Phee sat back suddenly. "They did that? For me? I just met Piper. I've known her a couple of weeks and she…she…"

"Piper said I could tell you this. She said to say that you and she have a lot in common and that sisters need to help each other out when one of them is in a bind. Does that make sense to you?"

Phee thought about it for a moment and then grinned. "She's trans too? Never had a clue. Holy cow! If you see them before I do, please tell her how much I appreciate what they did, okay?"

"I will, sweetie. Visiting hours are almost over. They are going to kick us out of here. Everything's going to be just fine, I know it will be."

"Okay, mom," she mumbled. "I shouldn't be tired, but I feel like I've run a marathon."

"Rest and we'll see you when you wake up. We'll come and drop off your things and maybe they'll let us see you for a few minutes then, okay?"

"I think she's already asleep, Mom," said Phee's sister.

Chapter 42

Piper parked the car outside The Gallery. Putting her hand into her pocket, she pulled out another of the Prince Rupert Tears. Handing the wrapped tear to her dad she said, "Dad, here is a Prince Rupert tear. Remember what we talked about? I think you should have one to keep."

He smiled as he slowly got out of the car. "I like that. So what is so important we needed to stop here first?"

"A surprise, an answer and a dream."

"A riddle? Okay, then. After the past few days, I guess I am up for almost anything. Lead on."

She led him around to the back. Emily answered the door and she asked them into the living room. Josh picked up the ancient cat, Sherry, and set her on the floor. Peter's book was on the coffee table.

After they'd been seated, Emily said, "Josh will be down in a moment. Can I get you something to drink?"

She brought them some tea and set Peter's down near the book.

He picked it up, holding it unopened. "I wrote this thirty some years ago."

"It's always been one of Josh's favorite books," Emily said. "It was the book that inspired him to become an artist."

Peter smiled. "Really? How about that." He opened it and read the inscription. His face paled and he didn't notice Josh stepping into the room.

"Laura."

"My mother," said Joshua. He sat on the couch next to Peter.

"Your... mother. I know that handwriting."

"I know," Josh said softly. "She was pregnant when she married my step-father. I grew up thinking I was his kid, but I found out, after he died, that I wasn't. I've been wondering about my real dad ever since."

"Dad," Piper interjected, "Look inside the back flap. Look at the picture."

He flipped the book over, hesitated, and then opened the back of the book. He stared at the picture of himself for a long moment before lifting his eyes and looking at Josh.

"I'm... you're... we..."

Josh nodded. He didn't say a word. He couldn't, his throat had closed up with emotions; fear, hope.

"I never knew. I didn't know she was pregnant. She didn't tell me. Why?"

Josh shrugged, his eyes on those of his father's, still waiting for something, anything.

"No one ever told him that part, Dad," Piper said softly. "All Josh knew was that the secret was hidden from him until after they both had died. His Grandmother Alice told him that the man he thought was his father, wasn't.

"I got a letter this morning from Alice (via her attorneys) explaining that you and Josh's mother were in love, but that something happened, she didn't know what, but that she thought I should know I had a brother. I don't expect that she ever thought it would be someone I already knew. That's why I received that money from her a while back. She felt that the questions and secrets needed to be shared."

Peter was still staring at Josh, into eyes so like his own. "We are… you are… I have…"

"Dad!" Piper was now on her feet. "You have a son and a daughter now!"

"I … have two children. Laura's child. Oh my God." He reached out to Josh who willingly gave his father a hug. Then putting his hands on Josh's shoulders, he backed away to just look at him. "I have so many questions. I tried to find her. I never understood why she went away or where. I would have been so happy to know we were to have a child."

Finally able to get words out, Josh said, "I don't guess we will ever know the answer to that. For me it is enough to know you both loved each other. My dad," he tried the words out. "I like the way that sounds," he said, choking a little.

"Me too," his father answered. "Laura is dead, then? How? When?"

"She died of cancer about five years ago. It was fast. She never let any of us know until right before the end. It was too late for chemo or anything. She passed almost immediately after telling us."

"You had brothers and sisters, then?"

"Yes, but we don't see each other. From the beginning, I was so different from them that we have never been close. Honestly, I don't even like them. They have their lives. I have mine. I'm okay with that. Especially," he grinned, "now!"

"I have a whole new family." Peter looked at Emily. "A daughter-in-law, too."

"Remember the riddle, Dad?"

"A surprise (I should say so!), an answer, and a dream."

"Here comes the answer to the dream." Looking over at Emily, she went and called into the other room. The three girls came shyly into the living room.

Josh stood. "Dad, I'd like you to meet our twins, Emma and Alice, and our youngest, Journey. Children, this man is your grandfather."

"Grandfather! I have a grampa!" Emma ran to give him a hug. Emily moved to shield him from the onslaught, but he shook his head.

"This does my heart more good than you can possibly know! Emma, is it?"

"Yes, Grampa. Auntie Jinn said that patience can pay off. I waited. And you came."

The other two children came forward and somehow, he managed to hug all three at once.

Piper and Josh stood, arms around each other, watching their father try to answer questions from the three girls all at the same time. "He's glowing," Piper said.

"So are we all, I think. I know you are," he answered.

Emily saw Sherry sit up, jump off the couch and run over to the sliding glass door and paw at the glass. Her eyes lifted. There, just inside, floated Jinn, her arm around an older woman. *Grandmother Alice?* The woman bent down to let her fingers move near the cat's head. Sherry batted her head the way cats do when being petted, and began purring. Straightening, Alice smiled at Emily for a moment. Then, her eyes roaming, she took in the entire family. 'Together, at last,' Emily heard her say before both Jinn and Grandmother Alice faded out of sight.

After a long, wonderful day, the kids were in bed. Emma waited patiently. When she saw Jinn she said, "I waited for you, Auntie Jinn. I thought you would come see me tonight. I have a grampa!"

"I know. And a new auntie."

"She's nice, but she isn't an angel like you are."

"I told you I am not an angel, Emma."

"To me, you are," Emma said firmly.

"Okay, okay. You win. She will love you, too, though. Remember that."

"I will. You came to say goodbye, didn't you?" Emma made a

pouty face.

"Yes, sweetheart. It is time for me to go. I love you all. Please tell your mom, I love her too."

"I will. I wish you didn't need to go."

"I wish I could stay too, but I can't. Be good, okay? Look out for your sisters."

"Do I have to?"

Jinn slanted her a look. "Okay, I promise," Emma said. "I love you, Auntie Jinn."

"I will always love you, too. Sleep now."

"Stay 'til I slee~~."

Jinn stayed as long as she was able, gently running her hand over Emma's head.

Chapter 43

Jinn watched as Josh and Emily took down the Jukai picture that had been hanging over the fireplace. Josh moved it to the opposite wall and then returned to help Emily place a new framed piece of artwork where it had been. Now, over the fireplace, painted in part from a recent photographic portrait of the family, were Peter, Piper, Josh, Emily and the three children, all grouped in a way that showed that they were indisputably together. A hand or an arm reaching out connected each to another, and, lying at Emma's feet, Sherry, Grandmother Alice's cat, licked a paw in satisfaction.

Jinn's eyes widened and she grinned. Behind the family, barely visible but still in the painting, were both Jinn and Grandmother Alice.

THE Annealing ~ AN EPILOGUE
THREE YEARS LATER

Piper had never made the glass piece to be used when giving Phee the 'Phoenix Fund' money. Once Phee'd been released from the hospital and returned to her apartment and told them she'd been cleared for the surgery (early, but there'd been a 'special circumstances leeway given), they just told her. Just like that. No fanfare, no big presentation. No one wanted to wait for the glass to be made.

Now they stood in the room that housed the permanent collection at The Gallery. Peter McAllister was there along with Josh, Emily and the children. Cee, her husband, Galen, Devon and Garret all stood there as well. In the past year, they had become one family. Today, Piper stood with Phee in front of a covered glass sculpture.

"I thought about this when I came up with the idea for the piece in the atrium," said Piper to Phee. "We all come from a gathering of glass. We start as molten bits and through our lives are formed into who we become. Life is a series of winds blowing us this way and that. Our lives are twisted and turned, the core of our beings constantly spinning. We encounter tears and we experience joys. From what we once were, we evolve. Like the glass, we have heated moments, fiery challenges, and cooling times when we stretch or are pulled.

"We here now are a gathering of friends who've become

family. A family of blood bonds and heart strings entangled with ribbons of overwhelming love.

"We've all experienced first-hand the utter joy of watching our own personal phoenixes rise from the ashes of what once was and seen them fly to new heights.

"Phee, this is for you, but more, for each of us. Not because we could ever forget, but because we will remember. It is in that remembering that we will always know to look beyond the people we encounter and to look deeply within and know their souls. We will see beyond masks and shells and into hearts and minds.

We will see and shall be seen."

"Phee, our resident Phoenix, through the film you had the courage to make and in which you star, you have shown the world a true vision of what the journey of a transgendered person entails. You have helped so many to have a glimmering of what we go through to finally be able to say, using author, Patti Dawn Swansson's words, 'I am complete.'"

With those final words, Piper drew the covering off the sculpture. In it, wings of fire spread wide, stood a phoenix just before taking flight. Red, yellow and orange feathers glowed as if with an interior light. Below it, in deep purples, blues and violets, were scattered tear shaped ashes.

"To think, all that magnificence began and was born... from a gathering of glass," said someone in an awed whisper.

Author's NOTES

This book could never have been written without the invaluable help of several individuals. Patti Dawn Swansson and Eris Katonic are two incredible transgender women. They were so very kind in putting up with all my questions. They both went out of their way to help me, and in turn, my readers, understand what being a transgender woman is all about. They were honest, forthcoming and gave me carte blanche to ask whatever I needed to ask. Their journeys are different and each is at a different way station. Each embraced the idea of more transgender people being in contemporary fiction, because, why shouldn't they be? Both of them, being writers, clearly understood how important it was for me to get my characters 'right.' We all share that the unknown can make some people fearful and if, in some small way, I can help people see that transgender people aren't sick, that being trans is not some form psychosis, but simply (although in no way simple) that their brains and all who they are doesn't match their outward body shells. I owe these women a debt I can never repay.

Another individual who shared her time, knowledge and expertise with me is April Wagner of Epiphany Glass Studio. (epiphanyglass.com) April spent hours showing me all the steps to create with glass, the various stages, types of glass, ovens and tools. She holds an Open House twice a year and the timing was such that I attended one of them as well and was able to create my own piece of glass art: the purple flower on the cover of this book! April creates phenomenal glass sculptures. Do check out her website!

No book is created from a vacuum. As an author I pull from people I meet, situations I encounter, places I go. C.M. Baker was the result of another inspiring and rising artist with a similar name. Her work (and the character's) in charcoal truly exists!

IF YOU ARE IN CRISIS: There are two important numbers available for anyone in a crisis situation.

NATIONAL SUICIDE PREVENTION LIFELINE
1 (800) 273-8255

THE TREVOR PROJECT LIFELINE
1 (866) 488-7386

Founded in 1998 by the creators of the Academy Award®-winning short film TREVOR, The Trevor Project is the leading national organization providing crisis intervention and suicide prevention services to lesbian, gay, bisexual, transgender and questioning (LGBTQ) young people ages 13-24.

A sneak peek at the beginning of the third book in The Journey Collection, *Masquerade*.

Prologue: MASQUERADE

Miss Annabelle Stewart wandered around her apartment on the ground floor of an old Victorian house that gazed down on San Francisco Bay. Dust motes danced in front of sparkling windows framed in long lace curtains. In her hand, she held a whiskey sour, freshly shaken, in a cut glass crystal tumbler, a prop from 'Mrs. Windermere's Ghost'. In the movie it held the poisoned draught that would send Mr. Windermere to the great beyond, but had been mixed up sending Mrs. Windermere instead. Annabelle thought it a fond joke to have snuck it out of the prop room and to be using each day for her libations.

Nothing much beats whiskey, she thought, absently running a perfectly manicured finger along a row of leather-bound books on one of the shelves that surrounded her fireplace. Donne, Shakespeare, Oscar Wilde, Chekhov, Noel Coward, Elliot and Miller. She smiled, thinking about her days walking the boards. Crinkling her nose, she thought about how there was a distinct smell to every stage; sweat, make-up, nerves, chalk.

Not, she thought, like the movies, though. Movies were different. Start, stop, again, again, this angle, stress that, move here instead, try this. Forgotten lines, stop, laugh, start again. So different from the stage where you never stopped no matter what!

Either way, what she'd loved most was sinking into whatever role she was playing. She loved playing the sirens and vamps in her heyday. She'd even loved playing the matriarchs, as she'd grown older: Queen Elizabeth II, Kathryn of Aragon, Marie Antoinette. It was so freeing to be whomever she was playing. She could escape into their world or, perhaps, she mused, she'd escaped this one.

Her eyes lit on the pile of old albums. Each, a deep mulberry leather, thick with black paper and filled with playbills and reviews. Pulling one from the shelf, she went over to sit in the high backed, winged, deeply velvet, huntress green chair. Her bichon, Dickon, hopped into her lap and as she opened the album, nudged her hand as if to say, "Pet me."

She did for a moment, finishing off the rest of her drink. Pushing the dog off to the side, she poured herself another, swirling it in the glass, hearing the ice cubes make that distinctive cocktail sound. Returning to her chair, she settled in and opened the album.

Richard Burton in Camelot. She'd understudied Julie Andrews, but never got to step on the stage. Immense shoes to step into, much as she'd have loved to spend one evening playing Guinevere to the only man who truly excelled as King Arthur. She'd never forget backstage after the third performance when she watched a young girl, perhaps six or seven, walk up to him and tug on his costume. Although he'd been involved in a discussion with the producer and the director, he'd turned, then bent his knee to be eye level with her. Even from halfway across the room she could hear the girl tell 'King Arthur' that she'd tell everyone the story of Camelot. Annabella had been teary eyed when he charged the girl to be a teller of tales and then, drawing Excalibur, as if he were knighting a man, told her he was making her a princess of Camelot forever and a day. She'd always wondered what became of that girl and if she had, indeed, become a teller of tales.

She finished her drink, considered another. She shrugged. Why the hell not? Her current companions wouldn't mind.

Returning, she continued turning pages. The playbill from Man of La Mancha. Oh, what a Dulcinea she'd been. And how handsome had been the men of the inn. Desmond LaFabre as Don Quixote, not so much. Miserable weasel of a man really. Good actor, lousy human being.

Ah, she smiled, running her finger over the face of 'Kiss Me' Kate. That was a role. Turning the page, she saw the program from a production of 'A Street Car Named Desire.' She could still hear Robert Fauntleroy's screaming 'Stella.' After one particularly horrid rehearsal, she remembered thinking she'd hear it in her nightmares for years! A few pages later, she stopped.

Who'd have thought that after all this time a photo of Frenchie could make her heart pound? Gulping down two swallows of her drink, she stared at his devilish good looks. Long, curly dark brown hair, like aged mahogany. That impish look in his eyes, that quirky smile that hinted at unparalleled romance or impending adventure. He wasn't French, had never been to France. His nickname came from the beret he always wore, his habit of using a cigarette holder and his inevitable black turtle necked sweaters. On the shorter side at only 5'8" he was muscular, narrow hipped and by god, what a dancer the man was. There wasn't an accent he couldn't do, a character he couldn't portray or a woman he couldn't make swoon at his feet. Yet he'd only had eyes for 'his Annie-bella.'

Sipping now, she turned the page to see the black bordered obituary.

AP—Los Angeles. Movie Stunt Tragedy

Star of stage and screen, Patrick 'Frenchie' O'Reilly, died today after a tragic accident. Known for always performing his own stunts, he'd been filming his final scene in the new block-buster, 'Fly High and Free' when the hot air balloon he was in crashed into the cliffs at Monterey Bay. Also injured in the accident was the balloon handler, Gary Reston. Monterey Police are investigating the accident and it appears that the balloon may have run out of fuel.

Mr. O'Reilly, star of numerous films was engaged to actress Annabelle Stewart. They had planned to wed after the film wrapped in a few weeks. Funeral services will be private with a cliff-side memorial possible.

Annabelle leaned her head back against the back of the chair, closed her eyes and let the memories of her Frenchie resurface. She'd never stopped loving him, never taken another lover nor been involved with anyone since. How could she? Surely no one could ever be all to her that he had been. He was the love of her life, her shining star, her heart-mate.

Dickon nudged at Annabella's hand, but she'd fallen asleep. Dickon lay his head down in her lap and slept as well. He didn't *really* need to go out.

ABOUT THE Author

Robin Moyer has been writing all her life and is the published author of five books and several plays that have gone on to production.

Robin is married, has a successful publishing company with over sixty authors, and lives in Michigan.